MARY

Books by Vladimir Nabokov

Ada, a novel

Bend Sinister, a novel

The Defense, a novel

Despair, a novel

Eugene Onegin, by Alexander Pushkin,
    translated from the Russian, with a Commentary

The Eye, a novel

The Gift, a novel

Invitation to a Beheading, a novel

King, Queen, Knave, a novel

Laughter in the Dark or *Camera Obscura*, a novel

Lolita, a novel

Mary, a novel

Nabokov's Dozen, a collection of short stories

Nabokov's Quartet, a collection of short stories

Nikolai Gogol, a critical biography

Pale Fire, a novel

Pnin, a novel

Poems

The Real Life of Sebastian Knight, a novel

The Song of Igor's Campaign, Anon.,
    translated from Old Russian

Speak, Memory or *Conclusive Evidence*, a memoir

Spring in Fialta and Other Stories

Three Russian Poets, verse translation from the Russian

The Waltz Invention, a drama

Translated from the Russian by Michael Glenny
in collaboration with the author

VLADIMIR NABOKOV

MARY

A NOVEL

McGraw-Hill Book Company · New York · Toronto

FIRST EDITION

07-045731-X

Library of Congress Catalog Card Number 71-126749

To Véra

Having recalled intrigues of former years,
having recalled a former love.

Pushkin

INTRODUCTION

The Russian title of the present novel, *Mashenka*, a secondary diminutive of *Maria*, defies rational transliteration (the accent is on the first syllable with the "a" pronounced as in "ask" and a palatalized "n" as in "mignon"). In casting around for a suitable substitute (*Mariette?*, *May?*) I settled for *Mary*, which seemed to match best the neutral simplicity of the Russian title name.

Mashenka was my first novel. I started working on it in Berlin, soon after my marriage in the spring of 1925. It was finished by the beginning of the following year and published by an émigré book company (Slovo, Berlin, 1926). A German version, which I have not read, appeared a couple of years later (Ullstein, Berlin, 1928). Otherwise, it has remained untranslated for the impressive span of forty-five years.

The beginner's well-known propensity for obtruding upon his own privacy, by introducing himself, or a vicar, into his first novel, owes less to the attraction of a ready theme than to the relief of getting rid of oneself, before going on to better things. It is one of the very few common rules I have accepted. Readers of my *Speak, Memory* (begun in the Nineteen-Forties) cannot fail to notice certain similarities between my recollections and Ganin's. His Mary is a twin sister of my Tamara, the ancestral avenues are there, the Oredezh flows through both books, and the actual photograph of the Rozhestveno house as it is today—beautifully reproduced on the cover of the Penguin edition (*Speak, Memory*, 1969)—could well be a picture of the pillared porch in the "Voskresensk" of the novel. I had not consulted *Mashenka* when writing Chapter Twelve of the autobiography a quarter of a century later; and now that I have, I am fascinated by the fact that despite the superimposed inventions (such as the fight with the village rowdy or the tryst in the anonymous town among the glowworms) a headier extract of personal reality is contained in the romantization than in the autobiographer's scrupulously faithful account. At first I wondered how that could be, how the thrill and the perfume could have survived the exigency of the plot and the ostentation of fictional characters (two of them even appear, very awkwardly, in Mary's letters), especially as I could not believe that a stylish imitation should be able to vie with plain truth. But the explanation is really quite simple: in terms of years, Ganin was three times closer to his past than I was to mine in *Speak, Memory*.

Because of the unusual remoteness of Russia, and because of nostalgia's remaining throughout one's life an insane companion, with whose heartrending oddities one is accustomed to put up in public, I feel no embarrassment in confessing to the sentimental stab of my attachment to my first book. Its flaws, the artifacts of innocence and inexperience, which any criticule could tabulate with jocose ease, are compensated for me (the sole judge in this case and court) by the presence of several scenes (convalescence, barn concert, boat ride) which, had I thought of it, should have been transported virtually intact into the later work. In those circumstances, I realized as soon as my collaboration with Mr. Glenny started that our translation should be as faithful to the text as I would have insisted on its being had that text not been mine. Revampments of the lighthearted and highhanded order that I used for the English version of, say, *King, Queen, Knave* could not be envisaged here. The only adjustments I deemed necessary are limited to brief utilitarian phrases in three or four passages alluding to routine Russian matters (obvious to fellow-émigrés but incomprehensible to foreign readers) and to the switch of seasonal dates in Ganin's Julian Calendar to those of the Gregorian style in general use (e.g., his end of July is our second week of August, etc.).

I must close this preface with the following injunctions. As I said in reply to one of Allene Talmey's questions in a *Vogue* interview (1970), "The best part of a writer's biography is not the record of his adventures but the story of his style. Only in that light can one properly assess the relationship, if any, between my first heroine and my recent Ada." I can as well say that there is none. The other remark concerns a bogus creed which is still being boosted in some quarters. Although an ass might argue that "orange" is the oneiric anagram of *organe*, I would not advise members of the Viennese delegation to lose precious time analyzing Klara's dream at the end of Chapter Four in the present book.

VLADIMIR NABOKOV
January 9, 1970

1

"Lev Glevo. Lev Glebovich? A name like that's enough to twist your tongue off, my dear fellow."

"Yes, it is," Ganin agreed somewhat coldly, trying to make out the face of his interlocutor in the unexpected darkness. He was annoyed by the absurd situation in which they both found themselves and by this enforced conversation with a stranger.

"I didn't ask for your name and patronymic just out of idle curiosity, you know," the voice went on undismayed. "I think every name—"

"Let me press the button again," Ganin interrupted him.

"Do press it. I'm afraid it won't do any good. As I was saying every name has its responsibilities. Lev and Gleb, now —that's a rare combination, and very demanding. It means you've got to be terse, firm and rather eccentric. My name is a more modest one and my wife's name is just plain Mary. By the way, let me introduce myself: Aleksey Ivanovich Alfyorov. Sorry, I think I trod on your foot—"

"How do you do," said Ganin, feeling in the dark for the hand that poked at his cuff. "Do you think we are going to be stuck here for long? It's time somebody did something. Hell."

"Let's just sit down on the seat and wait," the tiresome, cheerful voice rang out again just above his ear. "Yesterday when I arrived we bumped into each other in the passage. Then in the evening, through the wall, I heard you clearing your throat and I knew at once from the sound of your cough that you were a fellow countryman. Tell me, have you been boarding here for long?"

"Ages. Got a match?"

"No. I don't smoke. Grubby place, this *pension*—even though it is Russian. I'm a very lucky man, you know—my wife's coming from Russia. Four years, that's no joke. Yes, sir. Not long now. It's Sunday today."

"Damned darkness," muttered Ganin, and cracked his fingers. "I wonder what time it is."

Alfyorov sighed noisily, giving off the warm, stale smell of an elderly man not in the best of health. There is something sad about that smell.

"Only six more days now. I assume she's coming on Saturday. I had a letter from her yesterday. She wrote the address in a very funny way. Pity it's so dark, or I'd show it to you. What are you fumbling for, my dear fellow? Those little vents don't open, you know."

"For two pins I'd smash them," said Ganin.

"Come, come, Lev Glebovich. Wouldn't it be better to play some party game? I know some splendid ones, I make them up myself. For instance: think of a two-figure number. Ready?"

"Count me out," said Ganin, and thumped twice on the wall with his fist.

"The porter's been asleep for hours," droned Alfyorov's voice, "so it's no use banging like that."

"But you must agree that we can't hang here all night."

"It looks as if we shall have to. Don't you think there's something symbolic in our meeting like this, Lev Glebovich?

When we were on terra firma we didn't know each other. Then we happen to come home at the same time and get into this contraption together. By the way, the floor is horribly thin and there's nothing but a black well underneath it. Well, as I was saying, we stepped in without a word, still not knowing each other, glided up in silence and then suddenly—stop. And darkness."

"What's symbolic about it?" Ganin asked gloomily.

"Well, the fact that we've stopped, motionless, in this darkness. And that we're waiting. At lunch today that man—what's his name—the old writer—oh yes, Podtyagin—was arguing with me about the sense of this émigré life of ours, this perpetual waiting. You were absent all day, weren't you, Lev Glebovich?"

"Yes. I was out of town."

"Ah, spring. It must be nice in the country now."

Alfyorov's voice faded away for a few moments, and when it sounded again there was an unpleasant lilt to it, probably because the speaker was smiling.

"When my wife comes I shall take her out into the country. She adores going for walks. Didn't the landlady tell me that your room would be free by Saturday?"

"That is so," Ganin replied curtly.

"Are you leaving Berlin altogether?"

Ganin nodded, forgetting that nods were invisible in the dark. Alfyorov fidgeted on the seat, sighed once or twice, then began gently whistling a saccharine tune, stopping and starting again. Ten minutes passed; suddenly there came a click from above.

"That's better," Ganin said with a smile.

At the same moment the ceiling bulb blazed forth, and the humming and heaving cage was flooded with yellow light. Alfyorov blinked, as though just waking up. He was wearing an old sandy-colored, formless overcoat—of the so-called "in-between-season" sort—and holding a bowler hat. His thin fair hair was slightly ruffled and something about his features reminded one of a religious oleograph: that little golden beard, the turn of that scraggy neck from which he pulled off a bright-speckled scarf.

With a lurch the lift caught on the sill of the fourth-floor landing and stopped.

"A miracle," Alfyorov said, grinning, as he opened the door. "I thought someone had pressed the button and brought us up, but there's no one here. After you, Lev Glebovich."

But Ganin, with a grimace of impatience, gave Alfyorov a slight push and, having followed him out, relieved his feelings by noisily slamming the steel door behind him. Never before had he been so irritable.

"A miracle," Alfyorov repeated. "Up we came and yet there's no one here. That's symbolic too."

2

The *pension* was both Russian and nasty. It was chiefly nasty becaue all day long and much of the night the trains of the *Stadtbahn* could be heard, creating the impression that the whole building was slowly on the move. The hall, where there hung a bleary mirror with a ledge for gloves, and where stood an oak chest so placed that people naturally barked their shins on it, narrowed into a bare and very cramped passage. Along each side were three rooms, numbered with large black figures stuck onto the doors. These were simply leaves torn off a year-old calendar—the first six days of April, 1923. April 1—the first door on the left—was Alfyorov's room, the next was Ganin's, while the third belonged to the landlady, Lydia Nikolaevna Dorn, the widow of a German businessman who twenty years ago had brought her here from Sarepta and who the year before had died of brain fever. In the three rooms down the right-hand side—April 4 to 6—there lived Anton Sergeyevich Podtyagin, an old Russian poet; Klara, a full-busted girl with striking bluish-brown eyes; and, finally, in room 6 at the turn of the passage, two ballet dancers, Kolin and Gornotsvetov, both as giggly as women, thin, with powdered noses and muscular thighs. At the end of the first stretch of the passage was the dining room, with a lithograph of the Last Supper on the wall facing the door and the yellow, horned skulls of deer along another wall above a bulbous sideboard. On it stood two crystal vases, once the cleanest things in the whole apartment but now dulled by a coating of fluffy dust.

Upon reaching the dining room, the passage took a right-angled turn to the right. There, in tragical and malodorous depths, lurked the kitchen, a small room for the maid, a dirty bathroom and a narrow W.C., whose door was labeled with two crimson noughts deprived of the rightful digits with which they had once denoted two Sundays on Herr Dorn's desk calendar. A month after his death Lydia Nikolaevna, a tiny, slightly deaf woman given to mild oddities, had rented an empty apartment and turned it into a *pension*. In doing this she showed a singular, rather creepy kind of ingenuity in the way she distributed the few household articles she had inherited. The tables, chairs, creaking wardrobes and bumpy couches were divided among the rooms which she intended to let. Separated, the pieces of furniture at once faded, took on the inept, dejected look of a dismembered skeleton's bones. Her late husband's desk, an oaken monster with a cast-iron inkwell in the form of a toad and with a middle drawer as deep as a ship's hold, found its way to room 1, where Alfyorov now lived, while the revolving stool, originally bought to match the desk, was parted from it and led an orphaned existence with the dancers in room 6. A pair of green armchairs was also severed: one pined in Ganin's room, and the other one was used by the landlady herself or by her old dachshund, a fat black bitch with a gray muzzle and pendulous ears that had velvety ends like the fringes of a butterfly's wing. The bookshelf in Klara's room was adorned by the first few volumes of an encyclopedia, while the remaining volumes were allotted to Podtyagin. Klara had also been given the only decent washstand, with a mirror and drawers; in each of the other rooms there was simply a squat wooden prop and on it a tin basin and a jug of the same material. She had been forced, however, to buy additional beds. This caused Frau Dorn considerable pain, not because she was stingy, but because she had derived a kind of delicious thrill, a sense of pride in her own thrift, from the way she had distributed all her previous furniture. Now that she was a widow and her double bed too spacious for her to sleep in, she resented being unable to saw it up into the required number of parts. In a haphazard way she cleaned the rooms herself, but she had never been able to cope with food, so she kept a cook—the terror of the local market, a vast red-haired virago who on Fridays donned a crimson hat and sailed off for the northern quarters where she traded her blowsy charms. Lydia Nikolaevna was afraid of going into the kitchen and was altogether a quiet, timorous creature. Whenever her blunt-toed little feet brought her pattering along the corridor, the lodgers always had the feeling that this gray, snub-nosed little creature was not the landlady at all, but just some silly old woman who had strayed into someone else's apartment. Every morning, bent in half like a rag doll, she would hurriedly sweep the dust from under the furniture, then disappear into her room, the smallest of them all. There she would read tattered German books or look through her late husband's papers, whose contents she understood not a whit. The only other person to go into her room was Podtyagin, who would stroke her affectionate black dachshund, tickle its ears and the wart on its hoary muzzle, and try to make the dog sit up and proffer its crooked paw. He would talk to Lydia Nikolaevna about his senile aches and pains and about how he had been trying for six long months to get a visa to go to Paris where his niece lived, and where the long crusty loaves and the red wine were so cheap. The old lady would nod, occasionally questioning him about the other lodgers, in particular about Ganin, whom she found quite unlike all the other young Russians who had stayed in her *pension*. Having lived there for three months, Ganin was now preparing to leave, and had even said he would give up his room next Saturday; however, he had planned to leave several times before and had always changed his mind and put off his departure. Lydia Nikolaevna knew, from what the gentle old poet had told her, that Ganin had a girl friend. And there lay the root of the trouble.

Lately he had become dull and gloomy. Only a short while ago he could walk on his hands, quite as well as a Japanese acrobat, and with legs elegantly erect move along like a sail. He could pick up a chair in his teeth. He could break a string by flexing his biceps. His body was always burning with the urge to do something—to jump over a fence or uproot a post, in short to "bang," as we used to say when we were young. Now, however, some bolt had worked loose inside him, he had even acquired a stoop and he admitted to Podtyagin that he was suffering from insomnia "like a nervous female." He had an especially bad night from Sunday to Monday, after the twenty minutes spent with the effusive fellow in the stuck lift. On Monday morning he sat for a long time naked, gripping his cold, outstretched hands between his knees, appalled by the thought that today was another day and that he would have to put on shirt, trousers, socks—all those wretched things impregnated with sweat and dust—and he imagined a circus poodle which looks so ghastly, so sickeningly pitiful, when dressed up in human clothes. His inertia stemmed partly from his jobless state. He had no particular need to work at the moment, having saved that winter a certain amount of money; true, there was now no more than two hundred marks left of it: life had been rather expensive these last three months.

On arriving in Berlin last year he had at once found work and had worked until January at several different jobs. He had learned what it meant to go to work in a factory in the yellow murk of early morning; he had learned, too, how one's legs ached after trotting six sinuous miles a day carrying plates between the tables of the Pir Goroy restaurant; he had known other jobs too, and had sold every imaginable sort of goods on commission—Russian buns, and brilliantine, and just plain brilliants. Nothing was beneath his dignity; more than once he had even sold his shadow, as many of us have. In other words he went out to the suburbs to work as a movie extra on a set, in a fairground barn, where light seethed with a mystical hiss from the huge facets of lamps that were aimed, like cannon, at a crowd of extras, lit to a deathly brightness. They would fire a barrage of murderous brilliance, illumining the painted wax of motionless faces, then expiring with a click—but for a long time yet there would glow, in those elaborate crystals, dying red sunsets—our human shame. The deal was clinched, and our anonymous shadows sent out all over the world.

His remaining money was enough for him to leave Berlin, but that would mean shedding Lyudmila, and he did not know how to break with her. And although he had given himself a week to do it in and had told the landlady that he had finally decided to leave on Saturday, Ganin felt that neither this week nor the next would change anything. Meanwhile nostalgia in reverse, the longing for yet another strange land, grew especially strong in spring. His window looked out onto the railway tracks, so that the chance of getting away never ceased to entice him. Every five minutes a subdued rumble would start to move through the house, followed by a huge cloud of smoke billowing outside the window and blotting out the white Berlin daylight. Then it would slowly dissolve again, revealing the fan of the railway tracks that narrowed in the distance between the black, sliced-off backs of houses, all under a sky as pale as almond milk.

Ganin would have felt more at ease had he been living on

the other side of the corridor, in Podtyagin's room, or in Klara's; their windows looked out onto a rather dull street, and although it was crossed by a railway bridge it at least lacked the view into the pale, seductive distance. That bridge was a continuation of the tracks that could be seen from Ganin's window, and he could never rid himself of the feeling that every train was passing, unseen, right through the house itself. It would come in from the far side, its phantom reverberation would shake the wall, jolt its way across the old carpet, graze a glass on the washstand, and finally disappear out of the window with a chilling clang—immediately followed by a cloud of smoke billowing up outside the window, and as this subsided a train of the *Stadtbahn* would emerge as though excreted by the house: olive-drab carriages with a row of dark dog-nipples along their roofs and a stubby little locomotive coupled at the wrong end, moving briskly backward as it pulled the carriages into the white distance between blank walls, whose sooty blackness was either coming off in patches or was mottled with frescoes of outdated advertisements. It was as if an iron draft kept always blowing through the house.

"Ah, to leave!" muttered Ganin, stretching listlessly, and at once stopped short—what would he do about Lyudmila? It was absurd how flabby he had become. Once (in the days when he had walked on his hands or jumped over five chairs) he had been able not merely to control his will but to play games with it. There had been a time when he used to exercise it by making himself, for instance, get out of bed in the middle of the night in order to go down and throw a cigarette butt into a postbox. Yet now he could not bring himself to tell a woman that he no longer loved her. The day before yesterday she had stayed five hours in his room; yesterday, Sunday, he had spent the whole day with her on the lakes outside Berlin, unable to refuse her this ridiculous little excursion. Everything about Lyudmila he now found repulsive:

her yellow locks, fashionably bobbed, the two streaks of un-
shaven black hairs down the nape of her neck, her dark, languid eyelids, and above all her lips, glossy with purple-red
lipstick. He was bored and repelled when as she dressed, after
a bout of mechanical lovemaking, she would narrow her eyes,
which at once gave them an unpleasantly shaggy look, and
say, "I'm so sensitive, you know, that I shall be able to tell at
once when you don't love me as much as you used to." Ganin,
without replying, turned away toward the window, where
there rose a white wall of smoke. Then she would give a little
nasal snigger and call him in a husky whisper: "Come here."
At that moment he felt like wringing his hands to make the
joints crack in delicious pain, and say to her, "Get out,
woman, and goodbye." Instead of that he smiled and bent
down to her. She would run her nails, so sharp that they
might have been artificial, over his chest, and pout, and flutter
her coal-black eyelashes in her performance of a slighted girl
or a capricious marquise. There seemed to him something
sleazy, stale and old in the smell of her perfume, although she
herself was only twenty-five. As he brushed her hot little
forehead with his lips she forgot everything—forgot the falsity which she trailed around everywhere like her scent, the
falsity of her baby talk, of her exquisite senses, of her passion
for some imaginary orchids, as well as for Poe and Baudelaire,
whom she had never read; she forgot all her factitious charms,
her modishly yellow hair, sultry face powder and piggy-pink
silk stockings—and, tilting back her head, she would press
against Ganin her whole feeble, pathetic, unwanted flesh.

Bored and ashamed, Ganin felt a nonsensical tenderness—
a melancholy trace of warmth left where love had once fleet-
ingly passed by—which caused him to kiss without passion
the painted rubber of her proffered lips, although this tenderness did not succeed in silencing a calm, sarcastic voice advis-
ing him: try right now to thrust her away!

With a sigh he smiled gently down at her upturned face

and could think of nothing to say when she clutched him by the shoulder and begged him in a fluttery voice quite unlike her usual nasal whisper, her whole being seeming to fly into words, "Tell me—*please*—do you love me?" But as soon as she noticed his reaction—a familiar shadow, an involuntary frown—she remembered that she should be fascinating him with poetry, scent and sensibility, and at once began putting on her act that wavered between the poor little girl and the subtle courtesan. And again Ganin was seized with boredom, and he paced back and forth from the window to the door and back again, almost in tears from trying to yawn with his mouth shut while she put on her hat and watched him surreptitiously in the mirror.

Klara, a full-busted and very cosy young lady dressed in black silk, knew that her girl friend visited Ganin and she felt distressed and embarrassed whenever Lyudmila told her about her love affair. Klara considered that emotions of that kind ought to be more restrained, without violet irises and crying violins. But it was even more intolerable when her friend, narrowing her eyes and expelling cigarette smoke through her nostrils, would describe the still warm and horribly exact details, after which Klara would dream monstrous and shameful dreams. Lately she had taken to avoiding Lyudmila for fear that her friend would end by spoiling for her that enormous, always festive sensation that is daintily called "reverie." She loved Ganin's sharp, slightly arrogant features, his gray eyes with bright arrowlike streaks radiating from the unusually large pupils, his thick and very dark eyebrows which when he frowned or listened attentively formed a solid black line, but which unfurled like delicate wings whenever a rare smile momentarily bared his handsome, glistening teeth. Klara was so taken by these pronounced features that in his presence she lost her composure, did not say things she would have liked to say, constantly patted the wavy chestnut hair which half covered her ear, or rearranged the black silk folds on her bust, causing her lower lip to protrude and reveal her double chin. Anyway, once a day at lunch was the most she saw of Ganin, except for a single time when she had supper with him and Lyudmila in the squalid pub where he used to have his evening meal of würstchen and sauerkraut or cold pork. At lunch in the dreary *pension* dining room she used to sit opposite Ganin, as the landlady placed her lodgers at table in roughly the same order as the position of their rooms; thus Klara sat between Podtyagin and Gornotsvetov, and Ganin between Alfyorov and Kolin. The prim and sad little black figure of Frau Dorn seemed very out of place and forlorn at the head of the table between the facing profiles of the two affected, powdered ballet dancers, who spoke to her with little darting, birdlike quirks of demeanor. Hampered by her slight deafness, she herself spoke little and confined herself to seeing that the vast Erika brought in and cleared away the dishes at the proper time. Like a dry leaf her tiny wrinkled hand would now and then flit up to the dangling bell knob and then, yellow and faded, would flutter back again.

When Ganin entered the dining room at about half past two on Monday afternoon, all the others were already in their places. Catching sight of him, Alfyorov smiled in greeting and rose in his place, but Ganin did not offer his hand and sat down beside him with a silent nod, having already mentally cursed his obtrusive neighbor. Podtyagin, a neatly dressed, unassuming old man, who fed rather than ate, was noisily slurping his soup while with his left hand preventing his collar-lodged napkin from falling into the plate, glanced over the lenses of his pince-nez and then with a vague sigh returned to his slops. In a moment of frankness Ganin had told him about his oppressive love affair with Lyudmila and now regretted having done so. Kolin, on his left, passed him a plate of soup with tremulous care, giving him such an ingratiating look and such a smile with his strange veiled eyes that Ganin felt uncomfortable. Meanwhile, to his right, Alfyorov's unctuous little tenor voice resumed its prattling, objecting to something said by Podtyagin, who was sitting opposite him.

"You're wrong to find fault, Anton Sergeyevich. This is a most cultured country. No comparison with backward old Russia."

With a kindly glint of his pince-nez, Podtyagin turned to Ganin. "Congratulate me. Today the French have sent me my entrance visa. I feel like putting on the great ribbon of an order and calling on President Doumergue."

He had an unusually pleasant voice, soft, without change in pitch, mellow and mat in tone. His fat, smooth face with its gray little goatee under the lower lip and its receding chin seemed to be covered with an even, reddish tan, and wrinkles of kindliness fanned out around his serene, intelligent eyes. In profile he looked like a large, grizzled guinea pig.

"I'm so glad," said Ganin. "When are you leaving?"

But Alfyorov did not allow the old man to reply. Giving a habitual twitch to his scraggy neck with its sparse golden hairs and large mobile Adam's apple, he went on. "I advise you to stay here. What's wrong with this place? Things are straightforward here. France is more like a zigzag, and as for our Russia—that's a googly. I like it a lot here—there's work and the streets are nice for a walk. I can prove to you mathematically that if one's got to reside somewhere—"

"But," Podtyagin quietly interrupted him, "what about the mountains of paper, the coffinlike cardboard boxes, the interminable files, files and more files! The shelves are groaning under the weight of them. And the police official practically expired under the strain of finding my name in the records. You just can't imagine (at the word 'imagine' Podtyagin shook his head slowly and mournfully) what a person has to go through simply to be allowed to leave this country. As for the number of forms I've had to fill in! Today I had already begun to hope: ah, they will stamp my passport with their exit visa! Nothing of the sort. They sent me to have my picture taken, but the photos won't be ready until this evening."

"All very proper," Alfyorov nodded. "That's how things should be in a well-run country. None of your Russian inefficiency here. Have you noticed, for instance, what's written on the front doors? 'For the gentry only.' That's significant. Generally speaking, the difference between our country and this one can be expressed like this: imagine a curve, and on it—"

Ganin stopped listening and said to Klara, sitting opposite him, "Yesterday Lyudmila Borisovna asked me to tell you to ring her up as soon as you came home from work. It's about going to the cinema, I think."

Klara confusedly thought: "How can he talk about her so casually. After all, he knows that I know."

For propriety's sake she inquired, "Oh, did you see her yesterday?"

Ganin raised his eyebrows in surprise and went on eating.

"I don't quite understand your geometry," Podtyagin was saying, carefully sweeping breadcrumbs into the palm of his hand with his knife. Like most aging poets he had a penchant for plain human logic.

"But don't you see? It's so clear," cried Alfyorov excitedly. "Just imagine—"

"I don't understand it," Podtyagin repeated firmly, and, tilting his head back slightly, he poured the collection of crumbs into his mouth. Alfyorov spread out his hands in a gesture of helplessness and knocked over Ganin's glass.

"Oh, sorry!"

"It was empty," said Ganin.

"You're not a mathematician, Anton Sergeyevich," Alfyorov went on fussily, "but I've been swinging on that trapeze all my life. I once used to say to my wife that if I'm a 'summer' you're surely a spring cinquefoil—"

Gornotsvetov and Kolin dissolved in mannered mirth. Frau Dorn gave a start and looked at them both in fright.

"In short, a flower and a figure," said Ganin drily. Only Klara smiled. Ganin started pouring himself some water, his action watched by all the others.

"Yes, you're right, a most fragile flower," drawled Alfyorov, turning his bright, vacant look onto his neighbor. "It's an absolute miracle how she survived those seven years of horror. And I'm sure that when she arrives she'll be gay and blooming. You're a poet, Anton Sergeyevich; you ought to write something about it—about how womanhood, lovely Russian womanhood, is stronger than any revolution and can survive it all—adversity, terror—"

Kolin whispered to Ganin, "There he goes again—it was the same yesterday—all he could talk about was his wife."

"Vulgar little man," thought Ganin as he watched Alfyorov's twitching beard. "I bet his wife's frisky. It's a positive sin not to be unfaithful to a man like him."

"Lamb today," Lydia Nikolaevna suddenly announced stiffly, with a cross look at the listless way her lodgers were eating their meat course. Alfyorov bowed for some reason, then went on. "You're making a big mistake by not taking that as a theme." (Podtyagin was gently but firmly shaking his head.) "When you meet my wife perhaps you'll understand what I mean. She's very fond of poetry, by the way. You two ought to agree. And I'll tell you another thing—"

Glancing sidelong at Alfyorov, Kolin was stealthily beating time to him. Watching his friend's finger, Gornotsvetov shook with silent laughter.

"But the chief thing," Alfyorov burbled on, "is that Russia is finished, done for. She's been rubbed out, just as if someone had wiped a funny face off a blackboard by smearing a wet sponge across it."

"But—" Ganin smiled.

"Does what I say upset you, Lev Glebovich?"

"Yes, it does, but I won't stop you from saying it, Aleksey Ivanovich."

"Does that mean, then, that you believe—"

"Gentlemen, gentlemen," Podtyagin interrupted in his even, slightly lisping voice. "No politics, please. Why must we talk politics?"

"All the same, Monsieur Alfyorov is wrong," Klara put in unexpectedly, and gave her hair-do a brisk pat.

"Is your wife arriving on Saturday?" asked Kolin in an innocent voice down the length of the table, and Gornotsvetov tittered into his table napkin.

"Yes, Saturday," Alfyorov replied, pushing away his plate with the uneaten remains of his mutton. His eyes lost their combative gleam and immediately faded to a reflective look.

"Do you know, Lydia Nikolaevna," he said, "yesterday Lev Glebovich and I were stuck in the lift together."

"Stewed pears," replied Frau Dorn.

The dancers burst out laughing. Jogging the elbows of the people at table, Erika began to clear away the plates. Ganin carefully rolled up his napkin, squeezed it into its ring and stood up. He never ate dessert.

"What boredom," he thought as he made his way back to his room. "What can I do now? Go for a walk, I suppose."

The day, like the previous days, dragged sluggishly by in a kind of insipid idleness, devoid even of that dreamy expectancy which can make idleness so enchanting. Lack of work irked him now, but there was no work to do. Turning up the collar of his old mackintosh, bought for a pound from an English lieutenant in Constantinople (the first stage of exile), and thrusting his fists hard into its pockets, he strolled slowly

along the pale April streets, where the black domes of um-
brellas bobbed and swam. He stared long at a splendid model
of the *Mauretania* in a steamship company's window and at
the colored strings joining the ports of two continents on a
large map. At the back was a photograph of a tropical grove
—chocolate-brown palms against a beige sky.

He spent about an hour drinking coffee, sitting at a picture
window and watching the passers-by. Back in his room he
tried to read, but he found the contents of the book so alien
and inappropriate that he abandoned it in the middle of a
subordinate clause. He was in the kind of mood that he called
"dispersion of the will." He sat motionless at his table unable
to decide what to do: to shift the position of his body, to get
up and wash his hands, or to open the window, outside which
the bleak day was fading into twilight. It was a dreadful,
agonizing state rather like that dull sense of unease when we
wake up but at first cannot open our eyelids, as though they
were stuck together for good. Ganin felt that the murky twilight which was gradually seeping into the room was also
slowly penetrating his body, transforming his blood into fog,
and that he was powerless to stop the spell that was being cast
on him by the twilight.

He was powerless because he had no precise desire, and this
tortured him because he was vainly seeking something to desire. He could not even make himself stretch out his hand to
switch on the light. The simple transition from intention to
action seemed an unimaginable miracle. Nothing relieved his
depression, his thoughts slithered aimlessly, his heartbeat was
faint, his underclothes stuck unpleasantly to his body. At one
moment he felt he should at once write a letter to Lyudmila
explaining firmly that it was time to break off this dreary affair, then at the next he remembered that he was going to
the cinema with her that evening and that somehow it was
much harder to make himself ring her up and cancel today's

date than it was to write a letter, which prevented him from doing either.

How many times had he sworn to himself that he would break with her tomorrow and had had no trouble in concocting the appropriate things to say, only to fail utterly to visualize that final moment when he would press her hand and leave the room. It was that action—turning round, walking out—which seemed so unthinkable. He belonged to the sort of people who can get whatever they want, achieve, surpass; but he was quite incapable of renunciation or flight—which are, after all, one and the same thing. He was held back by a sense of honor and a sense of pity which blunted the will of a man who at other times was capable of any kind of creative enterprise, any exertion, and who would set about a task eagerly and willingly, cheerfully intent on overcoming everything and winning all.

He no more knew what kind of external stimulus would give him the strength to break off his three-month-old liaison with Lyudmila than he knew what was needed to get him up from his chair. Only for a very short time had he been genuinely in love—in that state of mind in which Lyudmila had seemed wreathed in a seductive mist, a state of questing, exalted, almost unearthly emotion, as when music plays at the very moment when one is doing something quite ordinary, such as walking from a table to pay at the bar, and gives an inward dancelike quality to one's simple movement, transforming it into a significant and immortal gesture.

That music had stopped at the moment one night when on the jolting floor of a dark taxi, he had possessed Lyudmila, and at once it had all become utterly banal—the woman straightening her hat that had slipped down onto the back of her neck, the lights flickering past the window, the driver's back towering like a black mountain behind the glass partition.

Now he was obliged to pay for that night with laborious deceit, to continue that night forever, and feebly, spinelessly yield to its creeping shadow that now filled every corner of the room, turning the furniture into clouds. He fell into a vague doze, his forehead propped on the palm of his hand and his legs stretched out stiffly under the table.

Later in the cinema it was crowded and hot. For a long time, colored advertisements for grand pianos, dresses, perfumes flocked silently across the screen. At last the orchestra struck up and the drama began.

Lyudmila was unusually cheerful. She had invited Klara to come too because she sensed very well that Klara was attracted to Ganin and she wanted to give pleasure to Klara, and to herself, by flaunting her affair and her ability to conceal it. Klara for her part agreed to come because she knew that Ganin was planning to depart on Saturday; also she was surprised that Lyudmila seemed not to know this—or else she purposely said nothing about it and was going to leave with him.

Sitting between them, Ganin was irritated because Lyudmila, like most women of her type, talked throughout the film about other things, bending across Ganin's knees toward her friend, every time dousing him in the chilling, unpleasantly familiar smell of her perfume. It was made worse by the fact that the film was thrilling and excellently done.

"Listen, Lyudmila Borisovna," said Ganin, unable to restrain himself any longer, "do stop whispering. The German behind me is starting to get annoyed."

She gave him a quick glance in the darkness, leaned back and looked at the bright screen.

"I don't understand a thing. It's pure rubbish."

"No wonder you can't understand it," said Ganin, "when you spend all the time whispering."

On the screen moved luminous, bluish-gray shapes. A prima donna, who had once in her life committed an involuntary murder, suddenly remembered it while playing the role of a murderess in opera. Rolling her improbably large eyes, she collapsed supine onto the stage. The auditorium swam slowly into view, the public applauded, the boxes and stalls rose in an ecstasy of approval. Suddenly Ganin sensed that he was watching something vaguely yet horribly familiar. He recalled with alarm the roughly carpentered rows of seats, the chairs and parapets of the boxes painted a sinister violet, the lazy workmen walking easily and nonchalantly like blue-clad angels from plank to plank high up above, or aiming the blinding muzzles of klieg lights at a whole army of Russians herded together onto the huge set and acting in total ignorance of what the film was about. He remembered young men in threadbare but marvelously tailored clothes, women's faces smeared with mauve and yellow make-up, and those innocent exiles, old men and plain girls who were banished far to the rear simply to fill in the background. On the screen that cold barn was now transformed into a comfortable auditorium, sacking became velvet, and a mob of paupers a theatre audience. Straining his eyes, with a deep shudder of shame he recognized himself among all those people clapping to order, and remembered how they had all had to look ahead at an imaginary stage where instead of a prima donna a fat, red-haired, coatless man was standing on a platform between floodlights and yelling himself to insanity through a megaphone.

Ganin's doppelgänger also stood and clapped, over there, alongside the very striking-looking man with the black beard and the ribbon across his chest. Because of that beard and his starched shirt he had always landed in the front row; in the intervals he munched a sandwich and then, after the take, would put on a wretched old coat over his evening dress and return home to a distant part of Berlin, where he worked as a compositor in a printing plant.

And at the present moment Ganin felt not only shame but

also a sense of the fleeting evanescence of human life. There on the screen his haggard image, his sharp uplifted face and clapping hands merged into the gray kaleidoscope of other figures; a moment later, swinging like a ship, the auditorium vanished and now the scene showed an aging, world-famous actress giving a very skillful representation of a dead young woman. "We know not what we do," Ganin thought with repulsion, unable to watch the film any longer.

Lyudmila was whispering to Klara again—something about a dressmaker and some stuff for a dress. The drama came to an end and Ganin felt mortally depressed. A few moments later as they were pushing their way toward the exit Lyudmila pressed close to him and whispered, "I'll ring you at two tomorrow, sweetie."

Ganin and Klara saw her home and then set off together back to their *pension*. Ganin was silent and Klara tried painfully to find a topic. "Are you going to leave us on Saturday?" she asked.

"I don't know, I really don't," Ganin replied gloomily.

As he walked he thought how his shade would wander from city to city, from screen to screen, how he would never know what sort of people would see it or how long it would roam round the world. And when he went to bed and listened to the trains passing through that cheerless house in which lived seven Russian lost shades, the whole of life seemed like a piece of film-making where heedless extras knew nothing of the picture in which they were taking part.

Ganin could not sleep. A nervous tingling ran through his legs and the pillow tormented his head. Then in the middle of the night his neighbor Alfyorov started to hum a tune. Through the thin wall he could hear him shuffling across the floor, first near then moving away, while Ganin lay there in anger. Whenever a train rattled past, Alfyorov's voice blended with the noise, only to surface again—tum-ti-tum, tum-ti, tum-ti-tum.

Ganin could bear it no longer. He pulled on his trousers, went out into the passage and thumped on the door of room 1 with his fist. In his wanderings Alfyorov happened at that moment to be right beside the door, and he flung it open so unexpectedly that Ganin gave a start of surprise.

"Please come in, Lev Glebovich."

He was wearing shirt and underpants, his blond beard was slightly ruffled—presumably from puffing away at his songs—and his pale blue eyes were alive with happiness.

"You're singing," said Ganin, frowning, "and it's keeping me awake."

"Come in for heaven's sake, don't hang about there in the doorway," fussed Aleksey Ivanovich, putting his arm round Ganin's waist in a well-meant but clumsy gesture. "I'm so sorry if I annoyed you."

Ganin went reluctantly into the room. It contained very little, yet was very untidy. Instead of standing at the desk (that oaken monster with the inkwell shaped like a large toad) one of the two kitchen chairs seemed to have wandered off in the direction of the washbasin but had stopped halfway there, having obviously stumbled over the turned-up edge of the green carpet. The other chair, which stood beside the bed and served as a bedside table, had disappeared under a black jacket whose collapse seemed as heavy and shapeless as if it had fallen from the top of Mount Ararat. Thin sheets of paper were scattered all over the wooden wilderness of the desk and over the bed. Ganin noticed from a casual glance that on these sheets were pencil drawings of wheels, squares, done without the least technical accuracy, simply scribbles to pass the time. Alfyorov himself, in his woollen underpants—which make any man, be he built like Adonis or elegant as Beau Brummel, look extraordinarily unattractive—had started pacing up and down again amidst the ruins of his room, occasionally flipping his fingernail against the green glass shade of the table lamp or the back of a chair.

"I'm terribly glad you've dropped in at last," he said. "I couldn't sleep either. Just think—my wife's coming on Saturday. And tomorrow's Tuesday already. Poor girl, I can just imagine what agony she's been through in that accursed Russia of ours!"

Ganin, who had been glumly trying to decipher a chess problem drawn on one of the pieces of paper lying around on the bed, suddenly looked up. "What did you say?"

"She's coming," Alfyorov replied with a bold flick of his nail.

"No, not that. What did you call Russia?"

"Accursed. It's true, isn't it?"

"I don't know—the epithet struck me as curious."

"Now, Lev Glebovich"—Alfyorov suddenly stopped in the middle of the room—"it's time you stopped playing at being a Bolshevik. You may think it very amusing, but what you do is very wrong, believe me. It's time we all admitted frankly that Russia is done for, that our 'saintly' Russian peasantry has turned out to be nothing but gray scum—as might have been expected, by the way—and that our country is finished for good."

Ganin laughed. "Quite, quite, Aleksey Ivanovich."

Alfyorov wiped his gleaming face from top to bottom with his palm and suddenly smiled a wide, dreamy smile. "Why aren't you married, old chap, eh?"

"Never had the chance," Ganin replied. "Is it fun?"

"Delightful. My wife is adorable. A brunette, you know, with such lively eyes. Still very young. We were married in Poltava in 1919, and in 1920 I had to emigrate. I've some photos in the desk drawer—I'll show them to you." Crooking his fingers underneath it, he pulled open the wide drawer.

"What were you in those days, Aleksey Ivanovich?" Ganin inquired without curiosity.

Alfyorov shook his head. "I don't remember. How can one

remember what one was in a past life—an oyster maybe, or a bird, let's say, or perhaps a teacher of mathematics? In any case our old life in Russia seems like something that happened before time began, something metaphysical or whatever you call it—that's not quite the word—yes, I know: metempsychosis."

Ganin looked at the photograph in the open drawer without much interest. It was the face of a tousled young woman with a merry, very toothy mouth. Alfyorov leaned over his shoulder. "No, that's not my wife, that's my sister. She died of typhus, in Kiev. She was a nice, jolly girl, very good at playing tag."

He produced another photograph.

"And that's Mary, my wife. Poor snapshot, but quite a good likeness all the same. And here's another, taken in our garden. Mary's the one sitting, in the white dress. I haven't seen her for four years. But I don't suppose she's changed much. I really don't know how I'll survive till Saturday. Wait! Where are you going, Lev Glebovich? Do stay!"

Ganin, his hands thrust into his trouser pockets, was walking toward the door.

"What's the matter, Lev Glebovich? Did I say something that offended you?"

The door slammed shut. Alfyorov was left standing alone in the middle of his room.

"Really! How rude," he mumbled. "What's bitten him?"

3

That night, as every night, a little old man in a black cape plodded along the curb down the long deserted avenue, poking the point of a gnarled stick into the asphalt as he looked for cigarette-ends—gold, cork or plain paper—and flaking cigar butts. Occasionally, braying like a stag, a motorcar would dash by or something would happen which no one walking in a city ever notices: a star, faster than thought and with less sound than a tear, would fall. Gaudier, gayer than the stars were the letters of fire which poured out one after another above a black roof, paraded in single file and vanished all at once in the darkness.

"Can—it—be—possible," said the letters in a discreet neon whisper, then the night would sweep them away at a single velvet stroke. Again they would start to creep across the sky: "Can—it—"

And darkness descended again. But the words insistently lit up once more and finally, instead of disappearing at once, they stayed alight for a whole five minutes, as had been arranged between the advertising agency and the manufacturer.

But then who can tell what it really is that flickers up there in the dark above the houses—the luminous name of a product or the glow of human thought; a sign, a summons; a question hurled into the sky and suddenly getting a jewel-bright, enraptured answer?

And in those streets, now as wide as shiny black seas, at that late hour when the last beer-hall has closed, and a native of Russia, abandoning sleep, hatless and coatless under an old mackintosh, walks in a clairvoyant trance; at that late hour down those wide streets passed worlds utterly alien to each other: no longer a reveler, a woman, or simply a passer-by, but each one a wholly isolated world, each a totality of marvels and evil. Five hackney droshkies stood on the avenue alongside the huge drumlike shape of a street *pissoir*: five sleepy, warm, gray worlds in coachman's livery; and five other worlds on aching hooves, asleep and dreaming of nothing but oats streaming out of a sack with a soft crackly sound.

It is at moments like this that everything grows fabulous, unfathomably profound, when life seems terrifying and death even worse. And then, as one swiftly strides through the nighttime city, looking at the lights through one's tears and searching in them for a glorious, dazzling recollection of past happiness—a woman's face, resurgent after many years of humdrum oblivion—all of a sudden, in one's mad progress, one is politely stopped by a foot passenger and asked how to get to such and such a street; asked in an ordinary voice, but a voice which one will never hear again.

4

Waking late on Tuesday morning, he felt some ache in his calves and, leaning his elbow on his pillow, he sighed once or twice, startled and amazed with the delight of it as he remembered what had happened that night.

The morning was a gentle, smoky white. The windowpanes shook with a businesslike rumble.

With a determined sweep he jumped out of bed and started shaving. Today this gave him a particular pleasure. People who shave grow a day younger every morning. Ganin felt that today he had become exactly nine years younger. Softened by flakes of lather, the bristles on his taut skin steadily crepitated as they fell to the little steel ploughshare of his safety razor. As he shaved Ganin moved his eyebrows and then, as he stood in the bathtub and doused his body in cold water from a jug, smiled with joy. He brushed his damp black hair, dressed quickly and went out.

None of the other lodgers spent their mornings in the *pension* except for the dancers, who usually did not get up until lunchtime. Alfyorov was away to see a friend with whom he was starting up some business, Podtyagin had gone to the police station to try and obtain his exit visa, while Klara, already late for work, was waiting for a tramcar on the corner, clutching to her chest a paper bag of oranges.

Very calmly Ganin climbed up to the second floor of a

familiar house and pulled the bell-ring. Opening the door but without removing the chain, a maid peeped out and said that Fräulein Rubanski was still asleep.

"I don't care, I must see her," said Ganin, and, pushing his hand into the gap, he unlatched the chain himself.

The maid, a pallid thickset girl, muttered indignantly, but Ganin elbowed her aside with the same firmness, marched into the semiobscurity of the corridor and knocked on a door.

"Who's there?" came Lyudmila's slightly hoarse morning voice.

"It's me. Open."

She pattered across the floor on bare feet, turned the key and, before looking at Ganin, ran to the bed and jumped back under the bedclothes. From the tip of her ear it was obvious that she was smiling, waiting for Ganin's approach.

But he stayed in the middle of the room and stood there for some time, clinking the small change in his mackintosh pockets.

Lyudmila suddenly turned onto her back and, laughing, opened her thin, bare arms. Morning did not suit her; her face was pale and puffy and her yellow hair stood on end.

"Well, come here," she pleaded and closed her eyes. Ganin stopped clinking his money.

"Look, Lyudmila," he said quietly. She sat up, her eyes open wide.

"Has something happened?"

Ganin stared hard at her and replied, "Yes. It seems I'm in love with somebody else. I've come to say goodbye."

She blinked her sleep-clogged eyelashes and bit her lip.

"That's all, really," said Ganin. "I'm very sorry, but it can't be helped. Let's say goodbye now. I think it will be better like that."

Lyudmila covered her face and fell back again face downward on the pillow. Her sky-blue quilt began slipping off sideways onto the fluffy white rug. Ganin picked it up and straightened it. Then he walked a couple of times back and forth across the room.

"The maid didn't want to let me in," he said.

Lyudmila lay buried in the pillow as if dead.

"She's never been exactly welcoming," said Ganin.

"It's time to turn off the heating. It's spring," he said a little while later. He walked from the door to the white full-length mirror, then put on his hat.

Lyudmila still did not move. He stood for a little longer, looked at her in silence and then, making a faint sound as though to clear his throat, he left the room.

Trying to tread quietly, he walked rapidly down the long passage, chose the wrong door and as he swung it open found himself in a bathroom, from which erupted a hairy arm and a leonine roar. He turned sharply around and after a further encounter with the dumpy maid, who was dusting a bronze bust in the hall, began to descend the low stone steps for the last time. The huge casement on the landing was wide open onto the back courtyard, and down in the yard an itinerant baritone was roaring a Russian Volga song in German.

Listening to that voice, vibrant as springtime itself, and glancing at the colored design on the open windowpane—a bunch of cubic roses and a peacock's fan—Ganin felt he was free.

He walked slowly along the street, smoking as he went. The day had a milky chill about it; ragged white clouds rose up before him in the blue space between houses. He always thought of Russia whenever he saw fast-moving clouds, but now he needed no clouds to remind him; since last night he had thought of nothing else.

The delightful private event which had occurred last night had caused the entire kaleidoscope of his life to shift and had brought back the past to overwhelm him.

He sat down on a bench in a public garden and at once the

gentle companion who had been following him, his gray vernal shadow, stretched out at his feet and began to talk.

Now that Lyudmila had gone he was free to listen.

Nine years ago. Summer of 1915, a country house, typhus. Recuperating from typhus was astonishingly pleasant. One lay as though on undulating air; one's spleen still ached occasionally, it was true, and every morning a hospital nurse, brought specially from Petersburg, wiped one's furry tongue —still sticky from sleep—with cotton wool soaked in port. The nurse was very short, with a soft bosom and small capable hands; she gave off a damp, cool, old-maidish smell. She loved to use folksy quips and the bits of Japanese which she remembered from the war of 1904. She had a peasant woman's face the size of a clenched fist, pock-marked, with a tiny nose; not a single hair ever peeped out from under her headdress.

One lay as though on air. To the left the bed was partitioned off from the doorway by a tawny cane screen with wavy curves. Close to him, in a corner to the right, stood the icon case: swarthy-faced images behind glass, wax candles, a coral crucifix. Of the two windows, the more distant one shone straight ahead, and the head of the bed seemed to be pushing itself from the wall while its foot aimed at that window with its brass knobs, each containing a bubble of sunlight; any moment it might be expected to take off, across the room, out into the deep July sky where puffy, bright clouds slanted upward. The second window, on the right-hand wall, gave on to a sloping pale-green roof: the bedroom was on the second floor and this was the roof of a single-story wing which contained the servants' quarters and the kitchen. At night the windows were closed on the inside with whitewashed folding shutters.

The door behind the screen led onto the staircase, while further along the same wall were a gleaming white stove and an old-fashioned washstand with a cistern and a beaklike tap;

you pressed a brass pedal with your foot and a thin fountain squirted out of the tap. To the left of the front window stood a mahogany chest of drawers with very stiff drawers, to the right of it a small ottoman.

The wallpaper was white with bluish roses. Sometimes, in semidelirium, one would fashion people's profiles out of these roses or wander up and down with one's eyes, trying not to touch a single flower or a single leaf on the way, finding gaps in the pattern, wriggling through, doubling back, landing in a blind alley and starting one's journey through the luminous maze all over again. To the right of the bed between the icon case and the side window hung two pictures—a tortoiseshell cat lapping milk from a saucer, and a starling made of real starling's feathers appliquéd above a drawing of a nesting box. Alongside, by the window frame, was fixed an oil lamp which had a knack of emitting a black tongue of soot. There were other pictures too: above the chest of drawers a lithograph of a barechested Neapolitan boy, and over the washbasin a pencil drawing of a horse's head with distended nostrils swimming in water.

All day long the bed kept gliding into the hot windy sky and when one sat up one saw the tops of the lime trees, sungilt from above, telephone wires on which swifts perched, and part of the wooden canopy over the red sandy drive where it led up to the front porch. Wonderful sounds came from outside—twittering, distant barking, a creaking pump.

One lay and floated and thought how one would soon be getting up: flies played in a pool of sun; and from Mother's lap by one's bedside a ball of colored silk, as though alive, jumped down and gently rolled across the amber-yellow parquet.

In this room, where Ganin had recuperated at sixteen, was conceived that happiness, the image of that girl he was to meet in real life a month later. Everything contributed to the creation of that image—the soft-tinted prints on the walls, the twittering outside the window, the brown face of Christ in the icon case, and even the washstand's diminutive fountain. The burgeoning image gathered and absorbed all the sunny charm of that room, and without it, of course, it would never have grown. It was after all simply a boyish premonition, a delicious mist, but Ganin now felt that never had such a premonition been so completely fulfilled. All Tuesday he wandered from square to square, from café to café, his memories constantly flying ahead like the April clouds across the tender Berlin sky. People sitting in the cafés supposed that this man staring so fixedly ahead must have some deep grief; on the street he carelessly bumped into people and once a fast car braked hard and swore, having nearly hit him.

He was a god, re-creating a world that had perished. Gradually he resurrected that world, to please the girl whom he did not dare to place in it until it was absolutely complete. But her image, her presence, the shadow of her memory demanded that in the end he must resurrect her too—and he intentionally thrust away her image, as he wanted to approach it gradually, step by step, just as he had done nine years before. Afraid of making a mistake, of losing his way in the bright labyrinth of memory, he re-created his past life watchfully, fondly, occasionally turning back for some forgotten piece of trivia, but never running ahead too fast. Wandering around Berlin on that Tuesday in spring, he recuperated all over again, felt what it was like to get out of bed for the first time, felt the weakness in his legs. He looked at himself in every mirror. His clothes seemed unusually clean, singularly ample, and slightly unfamiliar. He walked slowly down the wide avenue leading from the garden terrace into the depths of the park. Here and there the earth, empurpled by the shadows of leaves, broke into molehills that looked like heaps of black worms. He had put on white trousers and lilac socks, dreaming of meeting someone, not yet knowing who it would be.

Reaching the end of the avenue, where a white bench gleamed amid the dark greenery of fir needles, he turned back, and now far ahead in a gap between the lindens could be seen the orange-red sand of the garden terrace and the glittering panes of the veranda.

The nurse went back to Petersburg; leaning out of the carriage for a long while she waved her dumpy little arm and the wind worried her wimple. The house was cool, with spreads of sunlight here and there on the floor. Two weeks later he was already riding himself to exhaustion on his bicycle and playing Russian skittles in the evening with the son of the cowman. After another week the event he had been waiting for happened. "And where is it all now?" mused Ganin. "Where is the happiness, the sunshine, where are those thick skittles of wood which crashed and bounced so nicely, where is my bicycle with the low handlebars and the big gear? It seems there's a law which says that nothing ever vanishes, that matter is indestructible; therefore the chips from my skittles and the spokes of my bicycle still exist somewhere to this day. The pity of it is that I'll never find them again—never. I once read about the 'eternal return.' But what if this complicated game of patience never comes out a second time? Let me see—there's something I don't grasp— yes, this: surely it won't all die when I do? Right now I'm alone in a foreign city. Drunk. My head's buzzing from beer laced with cognac. I have tramped my fill. And if my heart bursts, right now, then my whole world bursts with it? Cannot grasp it."

He found himself again in the tiny public garden of the same square, but now the air had grown chilly, the pale sky had dimmed in a vesperal swoon.

"Four days left: Wednesday, Thursday, Friday, Saturday. And I might die any moment."

"Pull yourself together!" he mumbled abruptly, knitting his dark brows. "Enough of that. Time to go home."

On walking upstairs to the landing of the *pension*, he met Alfyorov, who, hunched in his voluminous overcoat and pursing his lips with concentration, was inserting a key into the keyhole of the lift.

"I'm going out to buy a newspaper, Lev Glebovich. Like to join me?"

"No, thanks," said Ganin, and went on to his room.

But as he grasped the door handle he stopped. A sudden temptation overcame him. He heard Alfyorov getting into the lift, heard the machine go down with its laborious dull din and heard the clang as it reached the bottom.

"He's gone," he thought, biting his lip. "Hell, I'll risk it."

Fate willed it that five minutes later Klara knocked on Alfyorov's door to ask him whether he had a postage stamp. The yellow light showing through the frosted glass upper panels of his door suggested that Alfyorov must be in his room.

"Aleksey Ivanovich," began Klara, simultaneously knocking and opening the door slightly, "do you have—"

She stopped short in amazement. Ganin was standing by the desk and hastily shutting the drawer. He looked round, teeth flashing, gave the drawer a push with his hip and straightened up.

"Good God," Klara murmured, and backed out of the room.

Ganin quickly strode after her, turning out the light and slamming the door as he went. Klara leaned against the wall in the semidarkness of the passage and looked at him with horror, pressing her chubby hands to her temples.

"Good God," she repeated in the same low voice. "How could you—"

With a slow rumble, panting after its exertions, the lift was rising again.

"He's coming back," whispered Ganin, with an air of mystery.

"Oh, I won't give you away," exclaimed Klara bitterly, her shining wet eyes fixed upon him. "But how could you? He's no better off than you are, after all. No, it's like a nightmare."

"Let's go to your room," said Ganin with a smile. "I'll explain if you like."

She detached herself from the wall and with head bowed led him to room April 5. There it was warm and smelled of good perfume; on the wall was a copy of Böcklins *The Isle of the Dead*, and on the table a framed photograph—Lyudmilas' face, very much retouched.

"We've quarreled." Ganin nodded toward the photograph. "Don't ask me in if she comes to see you. It's all over." Klara sat down with her feet up on a couch, wrapping herself in a black shawl.

"This is all nonsense, Klara," he continued, sitting down beside her and leaning on his outstretched arm. "Surely you don't really think I was stealing money, do you? Although of course I wouldn't like Alfyorov to find out that I was poking about in his desk."

"But what *were* you doing? What else could it be?" Klara whispered. "I didn't expect this of you, Lev Glebovich."

"What a funny girl you are," said Ganin. He noticed that her big, kind, somewhat prominent eyes were just a little overbright, that her shoulders were rising and falling rather too excitedly under her black shawl.

"Come, come." He smiled. "All right then, let's suppose I'm a thief, a burglar. But why should it upset you so much?"

"Please go," said Klara softly, turning her head away. He laughed and shrugged his shoulders.

When the door had closed behind him, Klara burst into tears and wept for a long time, the big shiny tears welling up rhythmically between her eyelashes and trickling in long drops down her cheeks, aglow with sobbing.

"Poor dear," she muttered. "What life has brought him to! And what can I say to him?"

There came a light tap on the wall from the dancers' room. Klara blew her nose hard and listened. The tap was repeated, velvety-soft and feminine: it was obviously Kolin tapping. Then there was a burst of laughter, someone exclaimed, "Alec, oh Alec, stop it," and two voices started a muffled, intimate conversation.

Klara thought how tomorrow, as always, she would have to go to work and hammer the keys until six o'clock, watching the mauve-colored line of type as it poured onto the page with a dry, staccato rattle; or how, if there was nothing to do, she would read, propping her borrowed and shamefully tattered book on her black Remington. She made herself some tea, listlessly ate her supper, then undressed, languidly and very slowly. Lying in bed she heard voices in Podtyagin's room. She heard somebody come in and go out, then Ganin's voice saying something unexpectedly loudly and Podtyagin answering in a low, depressed voice. She remembered that the old man had gone again today to see about his passport, that he suffered badly from heart trouble, that life was passing: on Friday she would be twenty-six. On and on went the voices—and it seemed to Klara she dwelt in a house of glass that was on the move, swaying and floating. The noise of the trains, although particularly audible on the other side of the corridor, could also be heard in her room, and her bed seemed to rise and sway. For a moment she visualized Ganin's back as he leaned over the desk and looked around over his shoulder, baring his bright teeth. Then she fell asleep and had a nonsensical dream: she seemed to be sitting in a tramcar next to an old woman extraordinarily like her Lodz aunt, who was talking rapidly in German; then it gradually turned out that it was not her aunt at all but the cheerful marketwoman from whom Klara bought oranges on her way to work.

5

That evening Anton Sergeyevich had a visitor. He was an old gentleman with a sandy moustache clipped in the English fashion, very dependable-looking, very dapper in his frock coat and striped trousers. Podtyagin was regaling him with Maggi's bouillon when Ganin entered. The air was tinged blue with cigarette smoke.

"Mr. Ganin—Mr. Kunitsyn." Anton Sergeyevich, breathing heavily, his pince-nez twinkling, gently pushed Ganin into an armchair.

"This, Lev Glebovich, is my old schoolfellow who once wrote cribs for me."

Kunitsyn grinned. "That's so," he said in a deep, rounded voice. "But tell me, my dear Anton Sergeyevich, what time is it?"

"Still early, time to sit a while yet."

Kunitsyn stood up, pulling down his waistcoat. "I can't, my wife's expecting me."

"In that case I have no right to detain you." Anton Sergeyevich spread his hands and glanced sidelong through his pince-nez at his visitor. "Please give my regards to your wife. I haven't the pleasure of knowing her, but give her my regards all the same."

"Thank you," said Kunitsyn. "Delighted. Goodbye. I believe I left my coat in the hall."

"I'll see you out," said Podtyagin. "Please excuse me, Lev Glebovich, I'll be back in a moment."

Alone, Ganin settled more comfortably in the old green armchair and smiled reflectively. He had called on the old poet because he was probably the only person who might understand his disturbed state. He wanted to tell him about many things—about sunsets over a highroad in Russia, about birch groves. He was, after all, that same Podtyagin whose verses were to be found beneath little vignettes in old bound volumes of magazines like *The World Illustrated* and *The Pictorial Review*.

Anton Sergeyevich returned, gloomily shaking his head. "He insulted me," he said, sitting down at the table and drumming on it with his fingers. "Oh, how he insulted me."

"What's the matter?" asked Ganin.

Anton Sergeyevich took off his pince-nez and polished it with the edge of the tablecloth.

"He despises me, that's what's the matter. Do you know what he said to me just now? He gave me one of his cold, sarcastic little smiles and he said, 'You've been spending your time scribbling poetry and I haven't read a word of it. If I had read it I would have wasted the time when I could have been working.' That's what he said to me, Lev Glebovich; I ask you—is that an intelligent thing to say?"

"What is he?" asked Ganin.

"Deuce knows. He makes money. Ah, well. You see, he's a person who—"

"But what's there to feel insulted about? He has one talent, you have another. Anyway, I'll bet you despise him too."

"But Lev Glebovich," Podtyagin fretted, "am I not right to despise him? It's not that which is so awful—the awful thing is that a man like him dares to offer me money."

He opened his clenched fist and threw a crumpled bank-note onto the table.

"And the awful thing is that I took it. Look and admire—twenty marks, God damn it."

The old man seemed to quiver all over, his mouth was opening and shutting, the little gray beard under his lower lip twitching, his fat fingers drumming on the table. Then he sighed with a painful wheezing sound and shook his head.

"Peter Kunitsyn. Yes, I still remember. He was good in school, the rascal. And always so punctual, with a watch in his pocket. During classes he used to hold up his fingers to show how many more minutes until the bell rang. Graduated from high school with a gold medal."

"It must be strange for you, remembering that," said Ganin pensively. "Come to think of it, it's even odd to remember some everyday thing—though really not everyday at all—something that happened a few hours ago."

Podtyagin gave him a keen but kindly look. "What's happened to you, Lev Glebovich? Your face looks somehow brighter. Have you fallen in love again? Yes, there is a strangeness about the way we remember things. How nicely you beam, dash it."

"I had a good reason for coming to see you, Anton Sergeyevich."

"And all I could offer you was Kunitsyn. Let him be a warning to you. How did *you* get on at school?"

"So-so," said Ganin, smiling again. "The Balashov academy in Petersburg—know it?" he went on, slipping into Podtyagin's tone of voice, as one often does when talking to an old man. "I remember the schoolyard. We used to play football there. There was firewood piled up under an archway and now and again the ball used to knock down a log."

"We preferred bat-and-tag, and cossacks-and-robbers,"

said Podtyagin. "And now life has gone," he added unexpectedly.

"Do you know, Anton Sergeyevich, today I remembered those old magazines which used to print your poetry. And the birch groves."

"Did you really?" The old man turned to him with a look of good-natured irony. "What a fool I was—for the sake of those birch trees I wasted all my life, I overlooked the whole of Russia. Now, thank God, I've stopped writing poetry. Done with it. I even feel ashamed at describing myself as 'poet' when I have to fill in forms. By the way, I made a complete mess of things again today. The official was even offended. I shall have to go again tomorrow."

Ganin looked at his feet and said, "When I was in the upper forms my schoolmates thought I had a mistress. And what a mistress—a society lady. They respected me for it. I didn't object, because it was I who started the rumor."

"I see," Podtyagin nodded. "There's something artful about you, Lyovushka. I like it."

"In actual fact I was absurdly chaste and felt none the worse for it either. I was proud of it, like a special secret, yet everybody thought I was very experienced. Mind you, I certainly wasn't prudish or shy. I was simply happy living as I was and waiting. And my schoolmates, the ones who used foul language and panted at the very word 'woman,' were all so spotty and dirty, with sweaty palms. I despised them for their spots. And they lied revoltingly about their amorous adventures."

"I must confess," said Podtyagin in his lacklustre voice, "that I began with a chambermaid. She was so sweet and gentle, with gray eyes. Her name was Glasha. That's the way it goes."

"No, I waited," said Ganin softly. "From the onset of puberty to sixteen, say, three years. When I was thirteen we were playing hide-and-seek once and I and another boy of the same age found ourselves hiding together in a wardrobe. In the darkness he told me that there were marvelous beauties who allowed themselves to be undressed for money. I didn't properly hear what he called them and I thought it was 'prinstitute'—a mixture of princess and young ladies' institute. So I had an entrancing, mysterious mental image of them. But then of course I soon realized how mistaken I had been because I saw nothing attractive about the women who strolled up and down the Nevski rolling their hips and called us high-school boys 'pencils.' And so after three years of proud chastity my wait came to an end. It was in summer, at our place in the country."

"Yes, yes," said Podtyagin. "I can see it all. Rather hackneyed, though. Sweet sixteen, love in the woods."

Ganin looked at him with curiosity. "But what could be nicer, Anton Sergeyevich?"

"Oh, I don't know, don't ask me, my dear chap. I put everything into my poetry that I should have put into my life, and now it's too late for me to start all over again. The only thought that occurs to me at the moment is that in the final reckoning it's better to have been sanguine by temperament, a man of action, and if you must get drunk do it properly and smash the place up."

"There was that too," Ganin smiled.

Podtyagin thought for a moment. "You were talking about the Russian countryside, Lev Glebovich. You, I expect, will probably see it again. But I shall leave my old bones here. Or if not here then in Paris. I seem to be thoroughly out of sorts today. Forgive me."

Both were silent. A train passed. Far, far away a locomotive gave a wild, inconsolable scream. The night was a cold blue outside the uncurtained windowpanes, which reflected the lampshade and a brightly lit corner of the table. Podtyagin sat hunched, his gray head bowed, twirling a leather cigarette case in his hands. It was impossible to tell what he was thinking about: whether it was about the dullness of his past life; or whether old age, illness and poverty had risen before his mind's eye with the same dark clarity as the reflection in the nighttime window; whether it was about his passport and about Paris; or whether he was thinking glumly that the pattern on the carpet exactly fitted round the toe of his boot, or how much he would like a glass of cold beer, or that his visitor had outsat his welcome—God knows. But as Ganin looked at his big drooping head, at the senile tufts of hair in his ears, at the shoulders rounded from writing, he felt such a sudden access of sadness that he lost all desire to talk about summer in Russia, about the pathways in the park, and least of all about the astonishing thing that had happened the day before.

"Well, I must go now. Sleep well, Anton Sergeyevich."

"Good night, Lyovushka," Podtyagin sighed. "I enjoyed our talk. You, at least, do not despise me for taking Kunitsyn's money."

Only at the last moment, in the doorway, did Ganin stop and say, "Do you know what, Anton Sergeyevich? I've started a wonderful affair. I'm going to her now. I'm very happy."

Podtyagin gave an encouraging nod. "I see. Give her my regards. I haven't the pleasure, but give her my regards all the same."

6

Strange to say he could not remember exactly when he had first seen her. Perhaps at a charity concert staged in a barn on the border of his parents' estate. Perhaps, though, he had caught a glimpse of her even before that. Her laugh, her soft features, her dark complexion and the big bow in her hair were all somehow familiar to him when a student medical orderly at the local military hospital (a world war was in full swing) had told him about this fifteen-year-old "sweet and remarkable" girl, as the student had put it—but that conversation had taken place before the concert. Now Ganin racked his memory in vain; he just could not picture their very first meeting. The fact was that he had been waiting for her with such longing, had thought so much about her during those blissful days after the typhus, that he had fashioned her unique image long before he actually saw her. Now, many years later, he felt that their imaginary meeting and the meeting which took place in reality had blended and merged imperceptibly into one another, since as a living person she was only an uninterrupted continuation of the image which had foreshadowed her.

That evening in July Ganin had pushed open the creaking iron front door and walked out into the blue of the twilight. The bicycle ran with special ease at dusk, the tire emitting a kind of whisper as it palpated each rise and dip in the hard earth along the edge of the road. As he glided past the darkened stables they gave off a breath of warmth, a sound of snorting and the slight thud of a shifting hoof. Further on, the road was enveloped on both sides by birch trees, noiseless at that hour; then like a fire smouldering on the threshing-floor a faint light shone in the middle of a field and dark streams of people straggled with a festive hum toward the lone-standing barn.

Inside a stage had been knocked up, rows of seats installed, light flooded over heads and shoulders, playing in people's eyes, and there was a smell of caramels and kerosene. A lot of people had turned up; the back was filled with peasant men and women, the dacha folk were in the middle, while in front, on white benches borrowed from the manorial park, sat about twenty patients from the military hospital in the village, quiet and morose, with hairless patches blotching the gray-blue of their very round, shorn heads. Here and there on the walls, decorated with fir branches, were cracks through which peeped the starry night as well as the black shadows of country boys who had clambered up outside on tall piles of logs.

The opera bass from Petersburg, a gaunt man with a face like a horse, gave forth a cavernal boom; the village school choir, obedient to the melodious flick of a tuning fork, joined in with the refrain.

Amid the hot yellow glare, amid the sounds that took on visible form in the folds of crimson and silvery headscarves, fluttering eyelashes, black shadows on the roof beams shifting whenever there was a puff of the night breeze, amid all this glitter and popular music, among all the heads and shoulders in the large, crowded barn, Ganin saw only one thing: he stared ahead at a brown tress tied with a black bow, slightly frayed at the edges, and his eyes caressed the dark, smooth, girlish sheen of the hair at her temple. Whenever she turned her face sideways to give the girl sitting beside her one of her

[45]

rapid smiling glances, he could also see the strong color in her cheek, the corner of a flashing, Tartar eye, the delicate curve of her nostril alternately stretching and tightening as she laughed. Later, when the concert was over, the Petersburg bass was driven away in the local mill owner's huge car which cast a mysterious light over the grass and then, with a sweep of its beam, dazzled a sleeping birch tree and the footbridge over a brook; and when the crowd of fair vacationists, in a festive flutter of white frocks, drifted away through the blue darkness across the dew-laden clover, and someone lit a cigarette in the dark, holding the flaring match to his face in cupped hands—Ganin, in a state of lonely excitement, walked home, the spokes of his bicycle clicking faintly as he pushed it by the saddle.

In one wing of the manor house, between the larder and the housekeeper's room, there was a spacious old-fashioned water closet; its window gave onto a neglected part of the garden where in the shade of an iron roof a pair of black wheels surmounted a well, and a wooden water trough ran over the ground between the bare, winding roots of three huge bushy poplars. The window was decorated by a stained-glass knight with a square beard and mighty calves, and he glowed strangely in the dim light of a paraffin lamp with a tin reflector which hung beside the heavy velvet cord. You pulled the cord and from the mysterious depths of the oaken throne there would come a watery rumbling and hollow gurgles. Ganin flung open the casement and installed himself, feet and all, on the window ledge; the velvet cord swung gently and the starry sky between the black poplars made you want to heave a deep sigh. And that moment, when he sat on the window ledge of that lugubrious lavatory, and thought how he would probably never, never get to know the girl with the black bow on the nape of her delicate neck, and waited in vain for a nightingale to start trilling in the poplars as in a poem by Fet—that moment Ganin now rightly regarded as the highest and most important point in his whole life.

He could not remember when it was he saw her next, whether it was the following day or a week later. At sunset, before evening tea, he had swung himself onto the wedge of sprung leather, had bent forward over the handlebars and ridden off straight into the western glow. He always chose the same circular route, through two hamlets divided by a pine wood, and then along the highway, between fields and back home through the big village of Voskresensk which lay on the river Oredezh, sung by Ryleev a century before. He knew the road by heart, now narrow and flat, with its compact margin running alongside a dangerous ditch, now paved with cobblestones which made his front wheel bounce, elsewhere scored with treacherous ruts, then smooth, pink and firm—he knew that road by feel and by sight, as one knows a living body, and he rode expertly along it, pressing resilient pedals into a rustling void.

The evening sun banded the rough trunks of a pine coppice with red fire; from dacha gardens came the knocking of croquet balls; midges kept getting into one's mouth and eyes.

Occasionally on the highway he would stop by a little pyramid of roadbuilding stone above which a telegraph pole, its wood peeling in grayish strips, gave off a gentle, desolate hum. He would lean on his bicycle, looking across the fields at one of those forest fringes only found in Russia, remote, serrated, black, while above it the golden west was broken only by a single long lilac cloud from under which the rays spread out like a burning fan. And as he stared at the sky and listened to a cow mooing almost dreamily in a distant village, he tried to understand what it all meant—that sky, and the fields, and the humming telegraph pole; he felt that he was just on the point of understanding it when suddenly his head would start to spin and the lucid languor of the moment became intolerable.

He had no idea where he might meet her or overtake her, at what turn of the road, in this copse or the next. She lived in Voskresensk and would go out for a walk in the deserted sunny evening at exactly the same time as he. Ganin noticed her from a distance and at once felt a chill round his heart. She walked briskly, blue-skirted, her hands in the pockets of her blue serge jacket under which was a white blouse. As Ganin caught up with her, like a soft breeze, he saw only the folds of blue stuff stretching and rippling across her back, and the black silk bow like two outstretched wings. As he glided past he never looked into her face but pretended to be absorbed in cycling, although a minute earlier, imagining their meeting, he had sworn that he would smile at her and greet her. In those days he thought she must have some unusual, resounding name, and when he found out from the same student that she was called Mary he was not at all surprised, as though he had known it in advance—and that simple little name took on for him a new sound, an entrancing significance.

"Mary," Ganin whispered, "Mary." He took a deep breath and held it, listening to the beating of his heart. It was about three o'clock in the morning, the trains did not run, and as a result the house seemed to have come to a standstill. On the chair, its arms flung out like a man struck rigid in the middle of a prayer, there hung in the darkness the vague white shape of his cast-off shirt.

"Mary," Ganin repeated again, trying to put into those two syllables all the music that they had once held—the wind, the humming of telegraph poles, the happiness—together with another, secret sound which gave that word its very life. He lay on his back and listened to his past. And presently from the next room came a low, gentle, intrusive tu-tu- tu-tu-: Alfyorov was looking forward to Saturday.

7

On the morning of the following day, Wednesday, Erika's rufous paw thrust itself into room April 2 and dropped a long mauve envelope onto the floor. With indifference Ganin recognized the big, sloping, very regular handwriting. The stamp had been stuck on upside down, and in one corner Erika's fat thumb had left a greasy imprint. Perfume permeated the envelope, and it occurred to Ganin in passing that scenting a letter was like spraying perfume on one's boots to cross the street. He filled his cheeks, blew out the air and pushed the unopened letter into his pocket. A few minutes later he took it out again, turned it around in his hands and threw it onto the table. Then he walked across the room a couple of times.

All the doors in the *pension* were open. The sounds of the morning housework mingled with the noise of the trains which took advantage of the drafts to rush through all the rooms. Ganin, who stayed at home in the mornings, generally swept up his own rubbish and made his bed. Now he suddenly realized that this was the second day that he had not cleaned up his room. He went out into the passage to look for a broom and a duster. Carrying a bucket, Lydia Nikolaevna scuttered past him like a mouse, and as she went by she asked, "Did Erika give you your letter?"

Ganin nodded in silence and picked up a long-handled brush that was lying on the oak chest. In the hall mirror he saw the reflection of the inside of Alfyorov's room, the door of which was wide open. Inside that sunny room—the weather that day was heavenly—a slanting cone of radiant dust passed across the corner of the desk, and with agonizing clarity he imagined the photographs which had first been shown to him by Alfyorov and which later he had been examining alone with such excitement when Klara had disturbed him. In those photos Mary had been exactly as he remembered her, and now it was terrible to think that his past was lying in someone else's desk.

The reflection in the mirror vanished with a slam as Lydia Nikolaevna, pattering down the corridor with her diminutive steps, pushed the door shut.

Floorbrush in hand, Ganin returned to his own room. On the table lay a mauve rectangle. By a rapid association of thought, evoked by that envelope and by the reflection of the desk in the mirror, he remembered those very old letters which he kept in a black wallet at the bottom of his suitcase, alongside the automatic pistol that he had brought with him from the Crimea.

He scooped up the long envelope from the table, pushed the window open wider with his elbow and with his strong fingers tore the letter crosswise, then tore up each portion and threw the scraps to the wind. Gleaming, the paper snowflakes flew into the sunlit abyss. One fragment fluttered onto the windowsill, and on it Ganin read a few mangled lines:

> ourse, I can forg
> ove. I only pra
> hat you be hap

He flicked it off the windowsill into the yard smelling of coal and spring and wide-open spaces. Shrugging with relief, he started to tidy his room.

Then one after another he heard his fellow lodgers returning for lunch, heard Alfyorov laugh aloud and Podtyagin softly mutter something. And a little while later Erika appeared in the passage and gave the gong a despondent bang.

On his way to lunch he overtook Klara, who gave him a frightened look. And Ganin smiled such a beautiful, kind smile that Klara thought: "So what if he is a thief—there's no one like him." Ganin opened the door, she lowered her head and walked past him into the dining room. The others were already sitting at their places, and Lydia Nikolaevna, holding an enormous ladle in her tiny withered hand, was sadly pouring out soup.

Podtyagin had been unsuccessful again today; the old man really had no luck. The French had allowed him in, but the Germans for some reason would not let him out. Meanwhile he only had just enough money left to make the journey, and if that foul-up lasted for another week he would have to spend his money on subsistence and then it would not be enough to get him to Paris. As he consumed his soup he described with a cheerless and ponderous jocularity how he had been chased from one department to another, how he had been unable to explain what he wanted, and how finally a tired and exasperated official had bawled him out.

Ganin looked up and said, "Let me come with you tomorrow, Anton Sergeyevich. I have plenty of time to spare. I'll help you to talk to them."

His German was, indeed, good.

"Why, thank you," Podtyagin replied, and he again noticed, as he had the day before, the unusual brightness of Ganin's expression. "It's enough to make one weep, you know. I spent two hours standing in a queue again and came back empty-handed. Thanks, Lyovushka."

"I expect my wife will be having trouble too," Alfyorov began. Something then happened to Ganin which had never happened to him before. He felt an intolerable blush slowly suffusing his face and tickling his forehead, as if he had drunk too much vinegar. Coming to lunch it had not occurred to him that these people, the ghosts of his dream-life in exile, would talk about his real life—about Mary. With horror and shame he recalled that in his ignorance the day before yesterday at lunch he had laughed with the others at Alfyorov's wife. And somebody might laugh again today.

"She's very efficient, though," Alfyorov was saying meanwhile. "She can stand up for herself. She knows how to look after herself, does my little wife."

Kolin and Gornotsvetov exchanged looks and giggled. Silently, sullenly, Ganin rolled a bread-ball. He almost got up and went out, but mastered himself. Raising his head he made himself look at Alfyorov, and having looked, was amazed how Mary could have married that person with the sparse little beard and shiny, plump nose. And the thought that he was sitting beside the man who had caressed Mary, who knew the feel of her lips, her jokes, her laugh, her movements, and who was now waiting for her—the thought was terrible, but with it he also felt a certain thrilling pride as he recalled that it had been to him and not her husband that Mary had first surrendered her profound, unique fragrance.

After lunch he went for a walk, then climbed up onto the top deck of a bus. Down below the streets poured by, little black figures dashed around on the shiny sunlit asphalt, the bus swayed and thundered—and Ganin felt that this alien city passing before him was nothing but a moving picture. As he returned home he saw Podtyagin knocking on Klara's door and Podtyagin too seemed to him a ghost, something extraneous and irrelevant.

"Our friend is in love with someone again." Anton Sergeyevich nodded toward the door as he drank tea with Klara. "It's not you, is it?"

Klara turned away; her ample bust rose and fell. She could

not believe it to be true; it frightened her, she was frightened by the Ganin who rifled other people's desks, but she was nevertheless pleased by Podtyagin's question.

"He's not in love with you, is he, Klarochka?" he repeated, blowing on his tea and giving her a sidelong glance over his pince-nez.

"He broke it off with Lyudmila yesterday," Klara said suddenly, feeling that she could reveal the secret to Podtyagin.

"I thought so," the old man nodded, sipping with relish. "He wouldn't be looking so radiant for nothing. Away with the old, on with the new. Did you hear what he suggested to me today? He's coming with me to the police tomorrow."

"I shall be seeing her this evening," said Klara reflectively. "Poor girl. She sounded deathly on the telephone."

Podtyagin sighed. "Ah, youth. That girl will get over it. No harm done. It's all for the best. As for me, Klarochka, I shall die soon."

"Good heavens, Anton Sergeyevich! What nonsense!"

"No, it's not nonsense. I had another attack last night. At one moment my heart was in my mouth, at the next moment it was under the bed."

"You poor man," said Klara anxiously. "You should see a doctor."

Podtyagin smiled. "I was joking. On the contrary, I've felt far better lately. And there was no attack. I invented it on the spur of the moment just to see your great eyes open still wider. If we were in Russia, Klarochka, some country doctor or a well-to-do architect would be courting you. Tell me—do you love Russia?"

"Very much."

"Quite so. We should love Russia. Without the love of us émigrés, Russia is finished. None of the people there love her."

"I'm already twenty-six," said Klara, "I type all morning,

and five times a week I work until six. I get very tired. I'm quite alone in Berlin. What do you think, Anton Sergeyevich —will it go on like this for long?"

"I don't know, my dear," sighed Podtyagin. "I'd tell you if I knew, but I don't. I worked too, I started up a magazine here. And now I've got nothing to show for it. I only hope to God I can get to Paris. Life's more free and easy there. What do you think—will I get there?"

"Why, of course you will, Anton Sergeyevich. Everything will be arranged tomorrow."

"Life's freer—and cheaper, apparently," said Podtyagin, spooning up an unmelted scrap of sugar and thinking that there was something Russian about that little porous lump, something rather like the melting snow in springtime.

8

In the sense of routine Ganin's day became emptier after his break with Lyudmila, but on the other hand he did not feel bored from having nothing to do. He was so absorbed with his memories that he was unaware of time. His shadow lodged in Frau Dorn's *pension*, while he himself was in Russia, reliving his memories as though they were reality. Time for him had become the progress of recollection, which unfolded gradually. And although his affair with Mary in those far-off days had lasted not just for three days, not for a week but for much longer, he did not feel any discrepancy between actual time and that other time in which he relived the past, since his memory did not take account of every moment and skipped over the blank unmemorable stretches, only illuminating those connected with Mary. Thus no discrepancy existed between the course of life past and life present.

It seemed as though his past, in that perfect form it had reached, ran now like a regular pattern through his everyday life in Berlin. Whatever Ganin did at present, that other life comforted him unceasingly.

It was not simply reminiscence but a life that was much more real, much more intense than the life lived by his shadow in Berlin. It was a marvelous romance that developed with genuine, tender care.

By the second week of August in northern Russia there is already a touch of autumn in the air. Every now and again a small yellow leaf falls from a birch tree; the broad fields, already harvested, have a bright autumnal emptiness. Along the forest's edge, where an expanse of tall grass spared by the haymakers shows its sheen to the wind, torpid bumblebees sleep on the mauve cushions of scabious flowers. And one afternoon, in a pavilion of the park—

Yes, the pavilion. It stood on rotting piles above a ravine, reached from either side by two sloping footbridges, slippery with alder aments and fir needles.

In its small diamond-shaped window frames were panes of different-colored glass: if, say, you looked through a blue one the world seemed frozen in a lunar trance; through a yellow one, everything appeared extraordinarily gay; through a red one, the sky looked pink and the foliage as dark as burgundy. Some of the panes were broken, their jagged edges joined up by a spider's web. Inside, the pavilion was whitewashed; vacationists who illegally wandered into the estate's park from their dachas had scribbled in pencil on the walls and on the folding table.

One day Mary and two of her rather plain girl friends wandered there too. He first overtook them on a path which ran alongside the river, and drove so close that her girl friends leaped aside with a shriek. He drove on round the park, cut through the middle and then from a distance through the leaves watched them go into the pavilion. He leaned his bicycle up against a tree and went in after them.

"This is private property," he said in a low, hoarse voice. "There's even a notice on the gate saying so."

She said nothing in reply, looking at him with her mischievous, slanting eyes. Pointing to one of the faint graffiti he inquired, "Did you do that?"

It said: "On the third of July Mary, Lida and Nina sat out a thunderstorm in this pavilion."

All three of them burst out laughing and then he laughed too. He sat on the window table, swinging his legs, and noticed with annoyance that he had torn one of his black socks at the ankle. Suddenly, pointing at the pink hole in the silk, Mary said, "Look—the sun has come out."

They talked about thunderstorms, about the people living in the dachas, about his having had typhus, about the funny student at the military hospital and about the concert.

She had adorable mobile eyebrows, a dark complexion with a covering of very fine, lustrous down which gave a specially warm tinge to her cheeks; her nostrils flared as she talked, emitting short laughs and sucking the sweetness from a grass stalk; her voice was rapid and burry, with sudden chest tones, and a dimple quivered at her open neck.

Then toward evening he escorted her and her friends to the village and as they walked down a green, weed-grown forest path, at the spot where stood a lame bench, he told them with a very straight face, "Macaroni grows in Italy. When still small it's called vermicelli. That means Mike's worms in Italian."

He arranged to take them all boating next day; but she appeared without her companions. At the rickety jetty he unwound the clanking chain of the rowboat, a big heavy affair of mahogany, removed the tarpaulin, screwed in the rowlocks, pulled the oars out of a long box, inserted the rudder pintle into its steel socket.

From some distance came the steady roar of the sluice gates at the water mill; one could distinguish the foamy folds of the falling water and the russet-gold sheen of pine logs that floated near.

Mary sat at the rudder. He pushed off with a boat hook and slowly started to row along the park shore where dense alder shrubs cast reflections like black eye-spots upon the water and many dark-blue demoiselle dragonflies flittered about. Then he turned into the middle of the river, weaving between the islets of algal brocade, while Mary, holding both ends of the tiller rope in one hand, dangled the other in the water trying to pull off the shiny yellow heads of waterlilies. The rowlocks creaked at every stroke of the oars and as he leaned back, then stretched forward, Mary, facing him in the stern, alternately moved away and drew closer in her navy-blue jacket, open over a light blouse that breathed with her.

The river now reflected the terra cotta of the left-hand bank, overgrown at the top with fir and racemosa. Names and dates had been cut in the red steep, and in one place ten years ago someone had carved a huge face with prominent cheek-bones. The right bank sloped gently, with purple patches of heather between dappled birch trees. And then cool darkness enveloped the boat under a bridge; from above came the heavy beat of hooves and wheels and, as the boat glided out, the dazzling sun flashed on the tips of the oars, and displayed the haycart crossing the low bridge and a green slope crowned by the white pillars of a boarded-up Alexandrine country mansion. Then a dark wood came down to the water's edge on both banks, and with a gentle rustle the boat sailed into the reeds.

No one at home knew about it, and life went on its dear, familiar summertime way hardly touched by the distant war which had now been in progress for a whole year. Linked to a wing by a gallery, the old greenish-gray wooden house with stained-glass windows in its twin verandas gazed out toward the fringe of the park, and at the orange, pretzel-shaped pattern of garden paths which framed the black-earth luxuriance of the flowerbeds. In the drawing room with its white furniture the marbled tomes of old bound magazines lay on the rose-embroidered tablecloth, the yellow parquet spilled out of a tilted mirror in an oval frame, and the daguerreotypes on the walls seemed to listen whenever the white upright piano tinkled into life. In the evening the tall blue-coated butler in cotton gloves carried a silk-shaded lamp out onto the veranda, and Ganin would come home to drink tea and to gulp cold curds-and-whey on that lighted veranda, with the rush mat on the floor and the black laurels beside the stone steps leading into the garden.

He now saw Mary every day on the far side of the river where the deserted white mansion stood on a green hill and where there was another park, larger and wilder than the one around the ancestral house.

In front of that other mansion, under the lime trees, on a broad terrace above the river, stood some benches and a round iron table with a hole in its center to drain off the rainwater. From there one could see far below a second bridge crossing a green-scummed bend in the river and the road leading up to Voskresensk. This terrace was their favorite spot.

Once, when they had met there on a sunny evening after a rainstorm, they noticed a swinish phrase scribbled on that garden table. Some village rowdy had linked their names by a short, crude verb, which moreover he had misspelled. The inscription had been done in indelible pencil and was slightly blurred by rain. Twigs, leaves and the chalky vermicules of bird-droppings were also sticking to the tabletop.

And since the table belonged to them, since it was sacred, sanctified by their meetings, they began calmly and without a word to rub out the damp scribble with tufts of grass. And when the whole surface had turned a ridiculous lilac color and Mary's fingers looked as if she had just been picking bilberries, Ganin, turning away and staring hard through narrowed eyes at a yellowy-green, warm, flowing something which at normal times was linden foliage, announced to Mary that he had been in love with her for a long time.

In those first days of love-making they kissed so much that Mary's lips grew swollen, and her neck, so warm under her hair-bow, bore tender vampire marks. She was an amazingly cheerful girl, who laughed not so much from mockery as from sheer humor. She loved jingles, catchwords, puns and poems. A song would stick in her head for two or three days, then it would be forgotten and a new one would take possession. During their first few meetings, for instance, she kept on soulfully repeating in her burry voice:

> Vanya's arms and legs they tied
> Long in jail was he mortified

and then she would say with her husky, crooning laugh, "Lovely song!" Around that time the last wild raspberries, rain-soaked and sweet, were ripening in the ditches. She was unusually fond of them, in fact she was more or less permanently sucking something—a stalk, a leaf, a fruit drop. She carried Landrin's caramels loose in her pocket, stuck together in lumps with bits of rubbish and wool sticking to them. She used a cheap, sweet perfume called "Tagore." Ganin now tried to recapture that scent again, mixed with the fresh smells of the autumnal park, but, as we know, memory can restore to life everything except smells, although nothing revives the past so completely as a smell that was once associated with it.

For a moment Ganin stopped recollecting and wondered how he had been able to live for so many years without thinking about Mary—and then he caught up with her again: she was running along a dark, rustling path, her black bow looking in flight like a huge Camberwell Beauty. Suddenly Mary pulled up, gripped him by the shoulder, lifted her foot and started to rub her sand-dusted shoe against the stocking of her other leg, higher up, under the hem of her blue skirt.

Ganin fell asleep lying dressed on top of his bedcover; his reminiscences had blurred and changed into a dream. The dream was odd and most precious, and he would have remembered it if only he had not been woken at dawn by a strange noise that sounded like a peal of thunder. He sat up and listened. The thunder turned out to be an incomprehensible groaning and shuffling outside the door; somebody was scraping at it. Gleaming very faintly in the dim dawn air, the door handle was suddenly pressed down and flicked up again, but although it was unlocked the door stayed shut. In pleasurable anticipation of adventure, Ganin slipped off his bed and, clenching his left fist in case of need, he flung open the door with his right hand.

In a sweeping movement, like a huge soft doll, a man fell prone against his shoulder. This was so unexpected that Ganin almost hit him, but he at once sensed that the man had only fallen on him because he was incapable of standing up. He pushed him aside toward the wall and fumbled for the light.

In front of him, leaning his head against the wall and gasping for air with his mouth wide open, stood old Podtyagin, barefoot, wearing a long nightshirt open at his grizzled chest. His eyes, bare and blind without their pince-nez, were unblinking, his face was the color of dry clay, the large mound of his stomach heaved beneath the taut cotton of his nightshirt.

Ganin immediately realized that the old man had been overcome by another heart attack. He supported him, and Podtyagin, moving his putty-colored legs with difficulty, tottered to a chair, collapsed into it and threw back his head; his gray face had now broken out in a sweat.

Ganin dipped a towel into his jug and pressed its heavy, wet folds to the old man's bare chest. He had a feeling that any moment all the bones in that big tense body might snap with a sharp crack.

Podtyagin took a breath and expelled the air with a whistle. It was not just a breath, but a tremendous pleasure which immediately caused his features to revive. With an encouraging smile Ganin continued to press the wet towel to his body and to rub his chest and sides.

"B—better," the old man breathed.

"Relax," said Ganin. "You'll be all right in a moment."

Podtyagin breathed and groaned, wriggling his large bare crooked toes. Ganin put a blanket round him, gave him some water to drink and opened the window wider.

"Couldn't—breathe," said Podtyagin laboriously. "Couldn't get into your room—too weak. Didn't want—die alone."

"Just relax, Anton Sergeyevich. It will be daylight soon. We'll call a doctor."

Podtyagin slowly wiped his brow with his hand and began to breathe more evenly. "It's gone," he said. "Gone for a while. I had no more of my drops left. That's why it was so bad."

"And we'll buy you some more drops. Would you like to move over into my bed?"

"No, I'll sit here a while and then go back to my room. It's gone now. And tomorrow morning—"

"Let's put it off until Friday," said Ganin. "The visa won't run away."

Podtyagin licked his dried lips with his thick, rough tongue. "They've been waiting for me in Paris for a long time, Lyo-vushka. And my niece hasn't got the money to send me any for the journey. Oh, dear!"

Ganin sat on the window ledge (in a flash he wondered where it was that he had sat like this not long ago—and in a flash he remembered: the stained-glass interior of the pavilion, the white folding table, the hole in his sock).

"Please put the light out, my dear fellow," Podtyagin asked him. "It hurts my eyes."

Everything seemed strange in the semidarkness: the noise of the first trains, the large, gray ghost in the armchair, the gleam of water spilled on the floor. And it was all much more mysterious and vague than the deathless reality in which Ganin was living.

9

It was morning and Kolin was making tea for Gornotsvetov. On that day, Thursday, Gornotsvetov had to leave town early in order to see a ballerina who was engaging a troupe. Everyone in the house, therefore, was still asleep when Kolin shuffled into the kitchen for hot water, wearing a remarkably dirty little kimono and battered boots on bare feet. His round, unintelligent, very Russian face with its snub nose and languorous blue eyes (he saw himself as Verlaine's "half Pierrot and half Gavroche") was puffy and shiny, his uncombed blond hair fell across his forehead, the untied laces of his boots pattered against the floor with a noise like fine rain. Pouting like a woman, he fiddled with the teapot and then began to hum quietly and intensely. Gornotsvetov was finishing dressing: he put on his polka-dotted bow tie, and lost his temper over a pimple which he had just nicked while shaving and which was now oozing pus and blood through a thick layer of powder. His features were dark and very regular, and long curled eyelashes gave his brown eyes a clear, innocent expression. He had short, black, slightly frizzled hair; he shaved the back of his neck like a Russian coachman and had grown sideburns which curved past his ears in two dark strips. Like his companion he was short, very thin, with highly developed leg muscles but narrow in the chest and shoulders.

They had made friends comparatively recently, had danced in a Russian cabaret somewhere in the Balkans and had arrived in Berlin two months ago in search of their theatrical fortune. A particular nuance, an odd affected manner set them somewhat apart from the other lodgers, but in all honesty no one could blame this harmless couple for being as happy as a pair of ringdoves.

Kolin, left alone in their untidy room after his friend had gone, opened a manicure case and, crooning softly, began to pare his fingernails. Although not remarkable for his cleanliness, he kept his nails in excellent condition.

The room reeked of Origan perfume and sweat; a ball of haircombings floated in the washbasin water. Ballet dancers pranced in photographs on the walls; on the table lay a large open fan and a dirty starched collar.

Having admired the coral varnish of his nails, Kolin carefully washed his hands, smeared his face and neck with sickly-sweet toilet water and threw off his dressing gown. Naked, he took a few steps on his points, did a little entrechat, quickly dressed, powdered his nose, and made up his eyes. Then, having fastened all the buttons of his gray, close-fitting topcoat, he went out for a walk flicking the tip of his fancy cane regularly up and down.

At the front door, as he returned home for lunch, he overtook Ganin, who had just bought some medicine for Podtyagin. The old man was feeling better; he was doing a little writing and walking about his room, but Klara, by agreement with Ganin, had decided not to let him out of the house that day.

Sneaking up behind him, Kolin gripped Ganin's arm above the elbow. Ganin turned round.

"Ah, Kolin. Had a good stroll?"

"Alec's away," said Kolin as he climbed the stairs beside

Ganin. "I'm terribly worried, I hope he's going to get that engagement."

"Yes, of course," said Ganin, who was always at a complete loss for conversation with him.

Kolin laughed. "Alfyorov got stuck in the lift again. Now it's not working."

He ran the knob of his cane along the banisters and looked at Ganin with a shy smile. "May I sit in your room for a bit? I'm so bored today."

"Don't imagine you can make eyes at me just because you're bored," Ganin mentally snapped at him as he opened the door of the *pension*, but aloud he said, "Unfortunately I'm busy at the moment. Some other time."

"What a pity," drawled Kolin, following Ganin inside and pulling the door after him. The door did not shut, as someone had thrust in a large brown hand from behind and a deep bass Berlin voice boomed, "One moment, gentlemen."

Ganin and Kolin looked round. A stout, mustachioed postman crossed the threshold.

"Does Herr Alfyorov live here?"

"First door on the left," said Ganin.

"Thank you," sang out the postman and knocked on the door he had been shown.

It was a telegram.

"What is it? What is it? What is it?" Alfyorov babbled feverishly, twisting it in his clumsy fingers. He was so excited that at first he was unable to read the glued-on strip of faint, uneven letters: ARRIVING SATURDAY 8 A.M. Suddenly Alfyorov understood, sighed and crossed himself.

"Thank the Lord. She's coming."

Smiling broadly and stroking his bony thighs, he sat down on the bed and started to rock backward and forward. His watery eyes were blinking rapidly, a slanting shaft of sun gilded his little dung-colored beard.

"*Sehr gut*," he muttered to himself. "The day after tomorrow! *Sehr gut.* What a state my shoes are in! Mary will be amazed. Still, we'll survive somehow. We'll rent a nice cheap little flat. She'll decide. Meanwhile we'll live here for a bit. Thank goodness there's a door between the two rooms."

A short while later he went out into the passage and knocked at his neighbor's.

Ganin thought, "Why can't they leave me alone today?"

Coming straight to the point, Alfyorov began as he surveyed the room all around, "I say, Gleb Lvovich, when are you thinking of leaving?"

Ganin looked at him with irritation. "My first name is Lev. Try and remember."

"But you are leaving on Saturday, aren't you?" Alfyorov asked, thinking to himself, "We'll have to place the bed differently. And the wardrobe must be moved away from the communicating door."

"Yes, I'm leaving," Ganin replied, and again, as at lunch the day before, he felt acutely embarrassed.

"Well, that's splendid," Alfyorov put in excitedly. "Sorry to disturb you, Gleb Lvovich."

And with a final glance round the room he went noisily out.

"Idiot," muttered Ganin. "To hell with him. What was I thinking about so delightfully just now? Ah, yes—the night, the rain, the white pillars."

"Lydia Nikolaevna! Lydia Nikolaevna!" Alfyorov's oily voice called loudly from the corridor.

"There's no getting away from him," thought Ganin angrily. "I won't lunch here today. Enough!"

The street asphalt gave off a violet gloss, the sun tangled with the wheels of motorcars. Near the beer-hall there was a garage and from the gaping gloom of its entrance came a tender whiff of carbide. And that chance exhalation helped Ganin to remember more vividly yet the rainy Russian late

August and early September, the torrent of happiness, which the specters of his Berlin life kept interrupting.

Straight out of the bright country house, he would plunge into the black, bubbling darkness and ignite the soft flame of his bicycle lamp; and now, when he inhaled that smell of carbide, it brought back everything at once: the wet grasses whipping against his moving leg and wheel spokes; the disk of milky light that imbibed and dissolved the obscurity; the different objects that emerged from it—now a wrinkled puddle, or a glistening pebble, then the bridge planks carpeted with horse dung, then, finally, the turnstile of the wicket, through which he pushed, with the rain-drenched pea-tree hedge yielding to the sweep of his shoulder.

Presently, through the streams of the night, there became visible the slow rotation of columns, washed by the same gentle whitish beam of his bicycle lamp; and there on the six-columned porch of a stranger's closed mansion Ganin was welcomed by a blur of cool fragrance, a blend of perfume and damp serge—and that autumnal rain kiss was so long and so deep that afterward great luminous spots swam before one's eyes and the broad-branching, many-leaved, rustling sound of the rain seemed to acquire new force. With rain-wet fingers he opened the little lantern's glass door and blew out the light. Out of the darkness a humid and heavy pressure of gusty air reached the lovers. Mary, now perched on the peeling balustrade, caressed his temples with the cold palm of her little hand and he could make out in the dark the vague outline of her soggy hairbow and the smiling brilliance of her eyes.

In the whirling blackness the strong, ample downpour surged through the limes facing the porch and drew creaks from their trunks, which were banded with iron clasps to support their decaying might. And amid the hubbub of the autumn night, he unbuttoned her blouse, kissed her hot clavicle; she remained silent—only her eyes glistened faintly, and the skin of her bared breast slowly turned cold from the touch of his lips and the humid night wind. They spoke little, it was too dark to speak. When at last he struck a match to consult his watch, Mary blinked and brushed a wet strand of hair from her cheek. He flung his arm around her while impelling his bicycle with one hand placed on its saddle, and thus they slowly walked away in the night, now reduced to a drizzle; first there was the descent along the path to the bridge, and then the farewell there, protracted and sorrowful, as though before a long separation.

And on the black stormy night, when on the eve of his return to St. Petersburg for the beginning of the school year they met for the last time on their pillared porch, something dreadful and unexpected occurred, a portent perhaps of all the desecrations to come. The rain that night was particularly noisy and their meeting especially tender. Suddenly Mary cried out and jumped down from the balustrade. By the light of a match Ganin saw that the shutter of one of the windows giving onto the porch was open, and that a human face, its white nose flattened, was pressed against the inside of the black windowpane. It moved and slithered away, but both of them had had time to recognize the carroty hair and gaping mouth of the watchman's son, a foulmouthed lecher of about twenty who was always crossing their path in the avenues of the park. In one furious leap Ganin hurled himself at the window, shattered the glass with his back and crashed into the icy dark. With this momentum his head butted a powerful chest, which gasped at the blow. Next moment they were grappling and rolling across the echoing parquet, bumping into dead pieces of furniture draped in dust covers. Freeing his right hand, Ganin began to slam his rocklike fist into the wet face which he suddenly found underneath him. He did not get up until the powerful body, which he had pinned to the floor, suddenly went slack and began to groan. Breathing hard, bumping against soft corners in the dark, he reached the window and climbed back onto the porch to find the sobbing, terrified Mary; he noticed then that something warm and tasting of iron was trickling out of his mouth and that his hands were cut by glass splinters. The next morning he left for St. Petersburg, and on the way to the station, in the closed carriage rolling along with a soft, muffled rumble, through the window he saw Mary walking on the edge of the road with her girl friends. The coachwork, lined with black leather, hid her immediately, and since he was not alone in the coupé he did not dare glance back through the oval rear peeper.

On that September day fate gave him an advance taste of his future parting from Mary, his parting from Russia.

It was a testing ordeal, a mysterious prevision; there was a peculiar sadness about the rowan trees, flame-red with fruit, receding one after another into the gray overcast, and it seemed incredible that next spring he would see those fields again, that lone boulder, those meditative telegraph poles.

At home in St. Petersburg everything seemed newly clean, bright and positive, as it always does when one returns from the country. School began again; he was in the penultimate form; he neglected his studies. The first snow fell, and the cast-iron railings, the backs of the listless horses and the barge-loads of firewood were covered with a thin layer of downy white.

Mary did not move to St. Petersburg until November. They met under the same arch where Liza dies in Tchai-kovsky's *The Queen of Spades*. Soft oversized snowflakes came down vertically in the gray, mat-glass air. At this, their first meeting in St. Petersburg, Mary seemed subtly different, perhaps because she was wearing a hat and a fur coat. From that day began the new, snowbound era of their love.

It was difficult to meet, long walks in the frost were agonizing, and finding a warm place to be alone in museums and cinemas was most agonizing of all. No wonder that in the frequent piercingly tender letters which they wrote to each other on blank days (he lived on the English Quay, she on Caravan Street) they both recalled the paths through the park, the smell of fallen leaves, as being something unimaginably dear and gone forever: perhaps they only did it to enliven their love with bittersweet memories, but perhaps they truly realized that their real happiness was over. In the evenings they rang each other up, to find out if a letter had been received, or where and how to meet. Her amusing *grasseyement* was even more attractive on the telephone; she would say truncated little poems, laugh warmly, and press the mouthpiece to her breast, and he imagined he could hear her heart beating.

They talked like this for hours.

That winter she wore a gray fur coat which made her look slightly plumper, and suede spats put on over her thin indoor shoes. He never saw her suffering from a cold, or even looking chilly. Frost or driving snow only vivified her, and in an icy snowstorm in some dark alleyway he would bare her shoulders; the snowflakes tickled her, she would smile through wet eyelashes, press his head to her, and a miniature snowfall would drop from his astrakhan cap onto her naked breast.

These meetings in the wind and frost tortured him more than her. He felt that their love was fraying and wearing thin as a result of these incomplete trysts. Every love demands privacy, shelter, refuge—and they had no such refuge. Their families did not know each other; their secret, which at first had been so wonderful, now hindered them. He began to feel that all would be well if she became his mistress, even if only in furnished rooms—and this thought somehow persisted in his mind apart from his feelings of desire, which were already weakening under the torment of their meager contacts.

So they roamed all winter, reminiscing about the country-side, dreaming of next summer, occasionally quarreling in fits of jealousy, squeezing each other's hands under the shaggy but scrimp rugs of cab drivers' sleighs; then early in the new year Mary was taken away to Moscow.

Strangely enough, this parting was a relief for Ganin.

He knew that in the summer she was planning to return to a cottage on his parents' land in the province of St. Peters-burg. At first he thought about it a lot, imagined a new sum-mer, new meetings, wrote her the same piercing letters and then began to write less often, and when his family moved to their country estate in mid-May he stopped writing alto-gether. Simultaneously he found time to make and break a liaison with an elegant and enchanting blond lady whose husband was fighting in Galicia.

Then Mary returned.

Her voice crackled weakly from a great distance, a noise hummed in the telephone as in a seashell, at times an even more distant voice on a crossed line kept interrupting, carry-ing on conversations with someone else in the fourth dimen-sion—the telephone in their country house was an old one with a hand crank—and between Mary and him lay thirty miles of roaring darkness.

"I'll come to see you," Ganin shouted into the receiver. "I'm saying I'll come. On my bicycle. It'll take a couple of hours."

"—didn't want to stay at Voskresensk again. D'you hear? Papa refused to rent a dacha at Voskresensk again. From your place to this town it's thirty—"

"Don't forget to bring those boots," interrupted a low, un-concerned voice.

Then Mary was heard again through the buzzing, in minia-ture, as if she were speaking from the wrong end of a tele-scope. And when she had vanished altogether Ganin leaned against the wall and felt that his ears were burning.

He set off at about three o'clock in the afternoon, in an open-necked shirt and football shorts, rubber-soled shoes on his sockless feet. With the wind behind him he rode fast, picking out the smooth patches between sharp flints on the highway, and he remembered how he used to ride past Mary last July before he even knew her.

After ten miles or so his back tire burst, and he spent a long time repairing it, seated on the edge of a ditch. Larks sang above the fields on both sides of the road; a gray convertible sped by in a cloud of gray dust, carrying two military men in owlish goggles. The tire mended, he pumped it up hard and rode on, aware that he had not allowed for this and was already an hour behind time. Turning off the highway he rode through a wood along a path shown to him by a passing muzhik. Then he took another turning, but a wrong one this time, and continued for a long while before getting back onto the right road again. He rested and had a bite to eat in a little village, and then, when he only had some eight miles to go, he ran over a sharp stone and once more the same tire expired with a whistle.

It was already getting dark when he reached the small town where Mary was spending the summer. She was waiting for him at the gates of the public park, as they had agreed, but she had already given up hope of his coming as she had been waiting since six o'clock. When she saw him she stumbled with excitement and almost fell. She was wearing a diaphanous white dress which Ganin did not know. Her black bow had gone, and, in result, her adorable head seemed smaller. There were blue cornflowers in her piled-up hair.

That night, in the strange stealthily deepening darkness, under the lindens of that spacious public park, on a stone slab sunk deep in moss, Ganin in the course of one brief tryst grew to love her more poignantly than before and fell out of love with her, as it seemed then, forever.

At first they conversed in a rapturous murmur—about the

long time they had not seen each other, about the resemblance of a glowworm that shone in the moss to a tiny semaphore. Her dear, dear Tartar eyes glided near his face, her white dress seemed to shimmer in the dark—and oh, God, that fragrance of hers, incomprehensible, unique in the world!

"I am yours," she said, "do what you like with me."

In silence, his heart thumping, he leaned over her, running his hands along her soft, cool legs. But the public park was alive with odd rustling sounds, somebody seemed to be continuously approaching from behind the bushes, the chill and the hardness of the stone slab hurt his bare knees; and Mary lay there too submissive, too still.

He stopped; then emitted an awkward short laugh. "I keep feeling that someone's around," said Ganin and got up.

Mary sighed, rearranged her dress—a whitish blur—and stood up, too.

As they walked back to the park gate along a moon-flecked path, she stooped over the grass and picked up one of the pale green lampyrids they had noticed. She held it upon the flat of her hand, bending over it, examining it closely, then burst out laughing and said in a quaint parody of a village lass, "Bless me, if it isn't simply a cold little worm."

It was then that Ganin, tired, cross at himself, freezing in his thin shirt, decided that it was all over, that he was no longer enamored of Mary. And a few minutes later, when he was cycling in the moonlight haze homeward along the pale surface of the road, he knew that he would never visit her again.

The summer passed; Mary did not write or telephone, while he was busy with other things, other emotions.

Once again he returned to St. Petersburg for the winter, took his final exams—earlier than was normal, in December—and entered the Mikhailov Officer Cadet School. Next summer, in the year of the revolution, he met Mary again.

It was toward evening and he was standing on the platform

at the Warsaw Station. The train taking holidaymakers out to their dachas had just pulled in. While waiting for the bell to ring he started to walk up and down the dirty platform. As he gazed at a broken luggage trolley he was thinking of something different, about the shooting that had taken place the day before on Nevski Avenue; at the same time he was annoyed that he had failed to get through to the family estate by telephone and that he would have to crawl all the way there from the station by droshky.

When the third bell clanged, he walked over to the only blue coach in the train, started to climb up to its vestibule—and there, looking down on him from above, stood Mary. She had changed in the past year, had grown perhaps slightly thinner and was wearing an unfamiliar blue coat with a belt. Ganin greeted her awkwardly, there was a clanging of buffers and the railway car moved. They remained standing in the vestibule. Mary must have seen him earlier and boarded a blue carriage on purpose, although she always traveled in a yellow one, and now with a second-class ticket she did not want to go inside into a compartment. She was holding a bar of Blighen and Robinson's chocolate, and at once broke off a piece and offered it to him.

It made Ganin terribly sad to look at her: there was something odd and timid in her whole appearance; she smiled less and kept turning her head away. On her tender neck there were livid marks, like a shadowy necklace, which greatly suited her. He spouted nonsense, showed her the scratch on his jackboot made by a bullet, talked about politics, while the train clattered on between peat-bogs burning in the tawny torrent of the sunset; the grayish peat smoke drifted gently over the ground, forming what seemed like two waves of mist between which the train clove its way.

She got off at the first station and for a long time he stared from the carriage platform after her departing blue figure, and the further away she went the clearer it became to him that he could never forget her. She did not look round. Out of the dusk came the heavy and fluffy scent of racemosa in bloom.

As the train moved off he went inside. There it was dark, the conductor having thought it unnecessary to light the lamp wicks in empty compartments. He lay down on his back on the striped cover of the couchlike seat and through the open door and the corridor window he watched thin wires rising through the smoke of burning peat and the dark gold of the sunset. There was something strange and spooky about traveling in this empty, rattling coach between streams of gray smoke, and curious thoughts passed through his head, as though this had all happened at some time before—as though he had lain there as now, his hands pillowing the back of his neck, in the drafty, clattering darkness, and the same smoky sunset had amply and sonorously swept past the windows.

He never saw Mary again.

10

The noise grew louder, flooded in, a pale cloud enveloped the window, a glass rattled on the washstand. A train had passed by and now the empty expanse of the railway tracks could be seen again fanning out from the window. Berlin, gentle and misty, toward evening, in April.

That Thursday at twilight, when the noise of the trains sounded hollower than ever, Klara came to see Ganin in a high state of agitation to give him a message from Lyudmila: "Tell him," Lyudmila had said, "tell him this: that I'm not one of those women that men can just drop. I'm the one who does the dropping. Tell him I don't want anything from him, I'm not making any demands, but I think it was filthy of him not to have answered my letter. I wanted to break it off with him in a friendly way, to suggest that even if we don't love each other any more we can simply be friends, but he couldn't even be bothered to ring me up. Tell him, Klara, that I wish him luck with his German girl and that I know he won't be able to forget me as quickly as he may think."

"Where on earth did she get the German girl from?" said Ganin, making a face, when Klara, without looking at him and talking in a low, rapid voice, had delivered her message. "Anyway, why does she have to involve you in this business? It's all very tiresome."

"You know, Lev Glebovich," Klara burst out, dousing him with one of her moist looks, "you really are heartless. Lyudmila thinks nothing but good of you, she idealizes you, but if she knew all about you—" Ganin looked at her with amiable astonishment. Embarrassed, Klara dropped her glance.

"I only gave you the message because she asked me to," Klara said quietly.

"I must leave," Ganin said after a silence. "This room, these trains, Erika's cooking—I'm fed up with it all. Besides, I'm nearly out of money and I shall have to work again soon. I'm thinking of leaving Berlin for good on Saturday, going south, to some sea port."

He clenched and unclenched his fist and lapsed into pensiveness.

"I don't know, though—there's one circumstance— You'd be amazed if you knew what has just occurred to me. An extraordinary, incredible plan! If it comes off I'll be out of this town by the day after tomorrow."

"Really, what a strange man he is," thought Klara, with that aching feeling of loneliness which always overcomes us when someone dear to us surrenders to a daydream in which we have no place.

Ganin's glassy black pupils dilated, his thick eyelashes gave his eyes a warm, downy look and a serene smile of contemplation lifted slightly his upper lip, baring the white expanse of his glistening, even teeth. His dark eyebrows, which reminded Klara of scraps of expensive fur, alternately met and parted, and soft furrows came and went on his smooth forehead.

Noticing Klara's stare, he blinked, passed his hand across his face and remembered what he had been intending to say to her. "Yes. I'm going, and that will end everything. Simply tell her that Ganin is leaving and wants her not to think ill of him. That's all."

11

On Friday morning the dancers sent round the following note to the other four lodgers:

Because:
1. Mr. Ganin is leaving us.
2. Mr. Podtyagin is preparing to leave.
3. Mr. Alfyorov's wife is arriving tomorrow.
4. Mlle. Klara is celebrating her twenty-sixth birthday
   and
5. The undersigned have obtained an engagement in this city— because of all this a celebration will be held tonight at 10 p.m. in room April 6th.

"How kind of them," said Podtyagin with a smile as he went out of the house with Ganin, who had agreed to accompany him to the police station. "Where are you going when you leave Berlin, Lyovushka? Far away? Yes, you're a bird of passage. When I was young I longed to travel, to swallow the whole wide world. Well, it's damn well happened—"

He hunched himself against the fresh spring wind, turned up the collar of his well-kept dark gray overcoat with its huge bone buttons. He still felt a debilitating weakness in the legs, an aftereffect of his heart attack, but today he derived a certain cheerful relief from the thought that now he would most likely have done with all the fuss about his passport and that he might even get permission to leave for Paris the very next day.

The vast purple-red building of the central police head-quarters faced onto four streets. It was built in a grim but extremely bad Gothic style with dim windows and a highly intriguing courtyard forbidden to the public; an impassive policeman stood at the main portal. An arrow on the wall pointed across the street to a photographer's studio, where in twenty minutes one could obtain a miserable likeness of one-self: half a dozen identical physiognomies, of which one was stuck onto the yellow page of the passport, another one went into the police archives, while the rest were probably distrib-uted among the officials' private collections.

Podtyagin and Ganin entered a wide gray corridor. At the door of the passport department stood a little table where an ancient bewhiskered official issued numbered tickets, occa-sionally casting a schoolmasterly glance over his spectacles at the small polyglot crowd of people.

"You must stand in the queue and get a number," said Ganin.

"And I never did that before," the old poet replied in a whisper. "I just used to go straight in through the door."

When he received his ticket a few minutes later he was de-lighted, and looked even more like a fat guinea pig than ever.

In the bare, stuffy, sunlit room where officials sat at their desks behind a low partition, there was another crowd which appeared to have come for the sole purpose of staring at those lugubrious scribes.

Ganin pushed his way through, with Podtyagin snuffling along trustfully after him.

Half an hour later, having handed in Podtyagin's passport, they moved over to another desk; again a queue, a crush of people, somebody's bad breath and, at last, for the price of a few marks the yellow sheet of paper was returned, now adorned with the magic stamp.

"Now off we go to the consulate," grunted Podtyagin joyfully as they left the redoubtable-looking though in reality rather dreary building. "It's in the bag now. How do you manage to talk to them so calmly, my dear Lev Glebovich? It was such agony for me when I went before! Come on, let's go on the top deck of the bus. What a joy this is—I'm actually in a sweat, you know."

He was the first to clamber up the twisting staircase. The conductor on the top deck banged on the iron side with his hand and the bus moved off. Houses, signboards, sunlight on shop windows floated by.

"Our grandchildren will never understand all this nonsense about visas," said Podtyagin, reverentially examining his passport. "They'll never understand that there could be so much human anxiety connected with a simple rubber stamp. Do you think," he added anxiously, "that the French really will give me a visa now?"

"Of course they will," said Ganin. "After all, they told you that permission had been given."

"I think I'll leave tomorrow," Podtyagin smiled. "Let's go together, Lyovushka. It'll be fine in Paris. No, you just look what a mug I have here."

Ganin glanced over his arm at the passport with its photograph in the corner. The photograph was quite remarkable: a dazed, bloated face swam in a grayish murk.

"I have no less than two passports," Ganin said with a smile. "One Russian, which is real but very old, and a Polish one, forged. That's the one I use."

As he paid the conductor, Podtyagin put down the yellow document on the seat beside him, selected 40 pfennigs from the several coins in his hand and glanced up at the conductor.

"*Genug?*"

He then looked sideways at Ganin.

"What did you say, Lev Glebovich? Forged?"

"Certainly. My first name really is Lev, but my surname is not Ganin at all."

"What do you mean, my dear fellow?" Podtyagin goggled in amazement and suddenly clutched at his hat—a strong wind was blowing.

"Well, that's the way it was," ruminated Ganin. "About three years ago. Partisan detachment. In Poland. And so on. Thought I'd break through to St. Petersburg and raise a rebellion. Now it's quite convenient and rather fun having this passport."

Podtyagin suddenly looked away and said glumly, "I dreamed about St. Petersburg last night, Lyovushka. I was walking along the Nevski. I knew it was the Nevski, although it looked nothing like it. The houses had sloping angles as in a futurist painting, and the sky was black, although I knew it was daytime. And the passers-by were giving me strange looks. Then a man crossed the street and took aim at my head. He's an old haunter of mine. It's terrible— oh, terrible—that whenever we dream about Russia we never dream of it as beautiful, as we know it was in reality, but as something monstrous—the sort of dreams where the sky is falling in and you feel the world's coming to an end."

"No," said Ganin, "I only dream about the beautiful things. The same woods, the same country house. Sometimes it's all rather deserted, with unfamiliar clearings. But that does not matter. We have to get out here, Anton Sergeyevich."

He went down the spiral staircase and helped Podtyagin to step onto the pavement.

"Just look at the way that water sparkles," Podtyagin remarked, breathing laboriously, and pointed at the canal with all five fingers stretched.

"Careful—mind that bicycle," said Ganin. "There's the consulate over there on the right."

"Please accept my sincere thanks, Lev Glebovich. If I'd

been on my own I'd never have got through all that red tape. It's a great relief to me. Farewell, Deutschland."

They entered the consulate building. As they went up the stairs Podtyagin began searching in his pockets.

"Come on," said Ganin, turning round.

But the old man kept searching.

12

Only four of the lodgers had turned up for lunch.

"I wonder why our friends are so late?" said Alfyorov cheerfully. "I suppose they've had no luck."

He positively breathed joyful expectation. On the previous day he had been to the station and found out the exact time of arrival of the morning fast train from the north: 8:05. To-day he had cleaned his suit, bought a pair of new cuffs and a bunch of lily-of-the-valley. His financial affairs appeared to have put themselves right. Before lunch he had sat in a café with a gloomy, clean-shaven gentleman who had offered him what was undoubtedly a money-making proposition. His mind, used as it was to figures, was now preoccupied with one single figure, made up of a unit and a decimal fraction: eight point zero five. This was the percentage of happiness which fate had temporarily allotted to him. And tomorrow—he screwed up his eyes, sighed and imagined how early tomorrow morning he would go to the station, how he would wait on the platform, how the train would come rushing in—

After lunch he disappeared, as did the dancers, who went out surreptitiously, as excited as two women, to buy little delicacies.

Only Klara stayed at home. Her head ached and the thin

bones of her fat legs were hurting, which was unfortunate, as today was her birthday. "I'm twenty-six today," she thought, "and tomorrow Ganin is leaving. He is bad, he deceives women and he is capable of committing a crime. He can look me calmly in the eyes even though he knows I saw him just about to steal money. Yet he's wonderful and I think about him literally all day. And there's no hope whatsoever."

She looked at herself in the mirror. Her face was paler than usual; beneath a lock of chestnut hair low down on her forehead she had broken out in a faint rash, and there were shadows under her eyes. She could not stand the glossy black dress which she wore day in, day out; there was a very obvious darn on the seam of her dark, transparent stocking; and one of her heels was crooked.

Podtyagin and Ganin returned around five o'clock. Klara heard their footsteps and looked out. Pale as death, his overcoat open and holding his collar and tie in his hand, Podtyagin walked silently past into his room and locked the door behind him.

"What's happened?" asked Klara in a whisper.

Ganin clicked his tongue. "He lost his passport, then he had an attack. Right here, in front of the house. I could hardly drag him upstairs. The lift's not working, unfortunately. We've been searching all over town."

"I'll go and see him," said Klara, "he'll need comforting."

Podtyagin would not let her in at first. When he finally did open the door, Klara groaned aloud when she saw his muzzy, confused expression.

"Have you heard?" he said with a wistful grin. "I am an old idiot. Everything was ready, you see—and then I have to go and—"

"Where did you drop it, Anton Sergeyevich?"

"That's it: I dropped it. Poetic license: elided passport. 'The Trousered Cloud' by Mayakovski. Great big clouded cretin, that's what I am."

"Perhaps somebody will pick it up," suggested Klara sympathetically.

"Impossible. It's fate. There's no escaping fate. I'm doomed not to leave here. It was preordained."

He sat down heavily.

"I don't feel well, Klara. I was so short of breath on the street just now that I thought it was the end. God, I simply don't know what to do now. Except perhaps kick the bucket."

13

Ganin meanwhile returned to his room and started to pack. From under the bed he pulled out two leather suitcases—one in a check cover, the other bare, tan-colored with pale marks left by labels—and spilled all the contents onto the floor. Then from the shaky, creaking darkness of the wardrobe he took out a black suit, a slender pile of underclothes, a pair of heavy, brass-studded brown boots. From the bedside table he extracted a motley collection of bits and pieces thrown in there at various times: dirty handkerchiefs crumpled into balls, razor blades with rusty stains around their eyelets, old newspapers, picture postcards, some yellow beads like horses' teeth, a torn silk sock which had lost its twin.

He took off his jacket, squatted down among all this sad, dusty rubbish and began to sort out what to take and what to destroy.

First he packed the suit and the clean underwear, then his automatic and a pair of old riding breeches, badly worn around the crotch.

As he pondered what to take next he noticed a black wallet that had fallen under the chair when he had emptied the suit-case. He picked it up and was going to open it, smiling as he thought of what was in it, but then he told himself that he should hurry up with his packing, so he thrust the wallet into the hip pocket of his trousers and began quickly throwing things at random into the open suitcases: crumpled dirty underclothes, Russian books which God alone knew how he had acquired, and all those trivial yet somehow precious things which become so familiar to our sight and touch, and whose only virtue is that they enable a person condemned to be always on the move to feel at home, however slightly, whenever he unpacks his fond, fragile, human rubbish for the hundredth time.

Having packed, Ganin locked both suitcases, stood them alongside each other, stuffed the wastepaper basket with the corpses of old newspapers, glanced all round his empty room and went off to settle up with the landlady.

Sitting bolt upright in an armchair, Lydia Nikolaevna was reading when he entered. Her dachshund slithered off the bed and began thrashing about in a little fit of hysterical devotion at Ganin's feet.

Lydia Nikolaevna saddened as she realized that this time he really was about to leave. She liked the tall, relaxed figure of Ganin; she generally tended to grow very used to her lodgers and there was something a little akin to death in their inevitable departures.

Ganin paid her for the past week and kissed her hand, light as a faded leaf.

As he walked back down the passage he remembered that today the dancers had invited him to a party and he decided not to go away just yet; he could always take a room in a hotel, even after midnight if necessary.

"And tomorrow Mary arrives," he exclaimed mentally, glancing round the ceiling, floor and walls with a blissful and frightened look. "And tomorrow I'm going to take her away," he reflected with the same inward shudder, the same luxurious sigh of his whole being.

With a quick movement he took out the black wallet in which he kept the five letters he had received during his time in the Crimea. Now in a flash he remembered the whole of that Crimean winter, 1917 to 1918: the nor'easter blowing the stinging dust along the Yalta seafront, a wave breaking over the parapet onto the sidewalk, the insolent and bewildered Bolshevik sailors, then the Germans in their helmets like steel mushrooms, then the gay tricolor chevrons—days of expectation, an anxious breathing space; a thin, freckled little prostitute with bobbed hair and a Greek profile walking along the seafront, the nor'easter again scattering the sheet music of the band in the park, and then—at last—his company was on the march: the billets in Tartar hamlets where all day long in the tiny barbers' shops the razor glittered just as it always had, and one's cheeks swelled with lather, while little boys in the dusty streets whipped their tops as they had done a thousand years ago. And the wild night attack when you had no idea where the shooting was coming from or who was leaping through the puddles of moonlight between the slanting black shadows cast by the houses.

Ganin took the first letter out of the bundle—a single, thick, oblong leaf with a drawing in the top left-hand corner that showed a young man in a blue tail coat holding behind his back a bouquet of pale flowers and kissing the hand of a lady, as delicate as he, with ringlets down her cheeks, wearing a pink, high-waisted dress.

That first letter had been forwarded to him from St. Petersburg to Yalta; it had been written just a little over two years after that blissful autumn.

"Lyova, I've been in Poltava for a whole week now, hellishly boring. I don't know if I shall ever see you again, but I do so want you not to forget me."

The handwriting was small and round, and looked exactly as if it were running along on tiptoe. There were strokes under the letter "щ" and above the letter "м̄" for clarity; the final letter of each word tailed off in an impetuous flick to the right; only in the letter " я " at the end of a word did the bar bend touchingly downward and to the left, as though Mary retracted the word at the last moment; her full stops were very large and decisive, but there were few commas.

"Just think, I've been looking at snow for a week, white cold snow. It's cold, nasty and depressing. And suddenly like a bird the thought darts through one's mind that somewhere far far away there are people living another completely different life. They're not stagnating as I am in the sticks, on a small farm.

"No, it's really too awfully dull here. Write me something, Lyova. Even the most absolute trifles."

Ganin remembered getting this letter, remembered walking up a steep stony path on that distant January evening, past Tartar picket fences hung here and there with horses' skulls, remembered how he sat beside a rivulet pouring in thin streams over smooth white stones, and stared through the countless, delicate and amazingly distinct bare branches of an apple tree at the mellow pink of the sky, where the new moon glistened like a translucent nail clipping, and beside it, by the lower horn, trembled a drop of brightness—the first star.

He wrote to her the same night—about that star, about the cypresses in the garden, about the donkey whose roaring bray came every morning from the Tartar yard behind the house. He wrote affectionately, dreamily, recalling the wet catkins on the slippery footbridge of the pavilion where they first met.

In those days letters took a long time on the way—the answer did not come until July.

"Thank you very much for your good, sweet, 'southern' letter. Why do you write that you still remember me? And you'll not forget me? No? How lovely!

"Today it's so nice and fresh, after a thunderstorm. As at Voskresensk—remember? Wouldn't you like to wander round those familiar places again? I would—terribly. How lovely it was to walk in the rain through the park in autumn. Why wasn't it sad then in bad weather?

"I'm going to stop writing for a while and go for a walk.

"I never did manage to finish the letter yesterday. Isn't that awful of me? Forgive me, Lyova dear, I promise I won't do it again."

Ganin dropped his hand with the letter and for a moment sat lost in thought. How well he remembered those merry mannerisms of hers, that husky little laugh when she apologized, that transition from a melancholy sigh to a look of ardent vitality!

"For a long time I was worried not knowing where you were and how you were," she wrote in the same letter. "Now we mustn't break off the little thread which links us. There's so much I want to write and ask you, but my thoughts wander. I've seen and lived through a lot of unhappiness since those days. Write, write for God's sake, write often and more. All the very best for now. I'd like to say goodbye more affectionately, but perhaps I've forgotten how to after all this time. Or perhaps there's something else holding me back?"

For days after getting that letter he was full of a trembling happiness. He could not understand how he could have parted from Mary. He only remembered their first autumn together —all the rest, those torments and tiffs, seemed so pale and insignificant. The languorous darkness, the conventional sheen of the sea at night, the velvety hush of the narrow cypress avenues, the gleam of the moonlight on the broad leaves of magnolias—all this only oppressed him.

Duty kept him in Yalta—the civil war was under way— but there were moments when he decided to give up everything to go and look for Mary among the farms of the Ukraine.

There was something touching and wonderful about the way their letters managed to pass across the terrible Russia of that time—like a cabbage white butterfly flying over the trenches. His answer to her second letter was very delayed, and Mary simply could not understand what had happened, as she was convinced that where their letters were concerned the usual obstacles of those days somehow did not exist.

"It must seem strange to you that I'm writing to you despite your silence—but I don't believe, I refuse to believe, that you still don't want to reply to me. You haven't replied, not because you didn't want to but simply because—well, because you couldn't, or because you hadn't time or something. Tell me, Lyova, doesn't it seem funny to remember what you once said to me—that loving me was your life, and if you couldn't love me you wouldn't be alive? Yes, how everything passes, how things change. Would you like to have what happened all over again? I think I'm feeling rather too depressed today . . .

> "But today it is spring and mimosa for sale
> At all corners is offered today.
> I am bringing you some; like a dream, it is frail—

"Nice little poem, but I can't remember the beginning or the end and I forget who wrote it. Now I shall wait for your letter. I don't know how to say goodbye to you. Perhaps I've kissed you. Yes, I suppose, I have."

Two or three weeks later came her fourth letter:

"I was glad to get your letter, Lyova. It is such a nice, nice letter. Yes, one can never forget how much and how radiantly one loved. You write that you would give your whole future life for a moment from the past—but it would be better to meet and verify one's feelings.

"Lyova, if you *do* come, ring up the local telephone exchange and ask for number 34. They may answer you in

German: there is a German military hospital here. Ask them to call for me.

"I was in town yesterday and had some 'fun.' It was very gay, with lots of music and lights. A very amusing man with a little yellow beard made a play for me and called me 'the queen of the ball.' Today it's so boring, boring. It's such a pity that the days go by so pointlessly and stupidly—and these are supposed to be the best, the happiest years of our life. It looks as if I shall soon turn into a hypocrite—I mean, hypochondriac. No, that mustn't happen.

> "Let me get rid of the shackles of love
> And let me try to stop thinking!
> Replenish, replenish the glasses with wine—
> Let me keep drinking and drinking!

"Quite something, isn't it?

"Write to me as soon as you get my letter. Will you come here and see me? Impossible? Well, too bad. Perhaps you can, though? What nonsense I'm writing: to come all the way here just to see me. What conceit! —don't you think?

"Just now I read a poem in an old magazine: 'My Little Pale Pearl' by Krapovitsky. I like it very much. Write and tell me absolutely everything. I kiss you. Here's something else I've read—by Podtyagin:

> "The full moon shines over forest and stream,
> Look at the ripples—how richly they gleam!"

"Dear Podtyagin," mused Ganin. "How strange. Goodness, how strange. If someone had told me then I should meet him, of all people."

Smiling and shaking his head, he unfolded one last letter. He had received it the day before leaving for the front line. It had been a cold January dawn on board ship, and he had felt queasy from drinking coffee made from acorns.

"Lyova, my darling, my joy, how I waited and longed for

your letter. It was so hard and painful to write you such restrained letters. How can I have lived these three years without you, how have I managed to survive and what was there to live for?

"I love you. If you come back I'll plague you with kisses. Do you remember:

> "Write to them that my little boy Lyov
> I kiss as much as I can,
> That an Austrian helmet from Lvov
> To bring for his birthday I plan
> But a separate note to my father—

"Goodness, where has it gone, all that distant, bright, endearing—Like you, I feel that we shall meet again—but when, when?

"I love you. Come to me. Your letter was such a joy that I still can't regain my senses for happiness—"

"Happiness," Ganin repeated softly, folding all five letters into an even batch. "That's it—happiness. We're going to meet again in twelve hours' time."

He stood motionless, preoccupied with secret, delicious thoughts. He had no doubt that Mary still loved him. Her five letters lay in his hand. Outside it was quite dark. The knobs on his suitcases gleamed. The desolate room smelled faintly of dust.

He was still sitting in the same position when voices were heard outside the door and suddenly, without knocking, Alfyorov strode into the room.

"Oh, sorry," he said without showing any particular embarrassment. "I somehow thought you'd already gone."

His fingers playing with the folded letters, Ganin stared vacantly at Alfyorov's little yellow beard. The landlady appeared in the doorway.

"Lydia Nikolaevna," Alfyorov went on, twitching his neck and crossing the room with a proprietorial air. "We must get this damn thing out of the way, so that we can open the door into my room."

He tried to move the wardrobe, grunted and staggered back helplessly.

"Let me do it," Ganin suggested cheerfully. Thrusting the black wallet into his pocket he stood up, walked over to the wardrobe and spat on his hands.

14

The black trains roared past, shaking the windows of the house; with a movement like ghostly shoulders shaking off a load, heaving mountains of smoke swept upward, blotting out the night sky. The roofs burned with a smooth metallic blaze in the moonlight; and a sonorous black shadow under the iron bridge awoke as a black train rumbled across it, sending a chain of light flickering down its length. The clattering roar and mass of smoke seemed to pass right through the house as it quivered between the chasm where the rail tracks lay like lines drawn by a moonlit fingernail and the street where it was crossed by the flat bridge waiting for the next regular thunder of railway carriages. The house was like a spectre you could put your hand through and wriggle your fingers.

Standing at the window of the dancers' room, Ganin looked out onto the street: the asphalt gleamed dully, black foreshortened people walked hither and thither, disappearing into shadows and re-emerging in the slanting light reflected from shop windows. In an uncurtained window of the house opposite, sparkling glass and gilded frames could be seen in the bright amber gap. Then an elegant black shadow pulled down the blinds.

Ganin turned around. Kolin handed him a quivering glassful of vodka.

The room was lit by a somewhat pale unearthly light, because the ingenious dancers had shrouded the lamp in a scrap of mauve silk. On the table, in the middle of the room, bottles gave off a violet-colored gleam, oil glistened in open sardine tins, there were chocolates in silver wrappings, a mosaic of sausage slices, glazed meat patties.

Sitting at the table were Podtyagin, pale and morose, with beads of sweat on his large forehead; Alfyorov, sporting a brand new shot-silk tie; Klara in her eternal black dress, languid and flushed from drinking cheap orange liqueur.

Gornotsvetov, without a jacket and wearing a soiled silk shirt with an open collar, was sitting on the edge of the bed tuning a guitar which he had somehow obtained. Kolin kept constantly on the move pouring out vodka, liqueurs, pale Rhine wine, his fat hips wriggling comically while his trim torso, gripped by a tight blue jacket, remained almost motionless as he moved.

"What—not drinking?" he pouted, asking the conventional reproachful question as he raised his melting glance to Ganin.

"Yes—why not?" said Ganin, sitting down on the window ledge and taking the light, cold wineglass from the dancer's trembling hand. Tossing it down, he glanced round the people sitting at the table. All were silent—even Alfyorov who was much too excited by the fact that in eight or nine hours' time his wife would arrive.

"The guitar's in tune," said Gornotsvetov as he adjusted a key and plucked the string. He struck a chord, then damped the twanging sound with his palm.

"Why aren't you singing, gentlemen? In Klara's honor. Come along now. 'Like a fragrant flower—' "

Grinning at Klara and raising his glass with mock gallantry, Alfyorov leaned backward in his chair—at which he nearly fell over, as it was a revolving stool without a back—and made an effort to sing in a false, affected little tenor, but no one else joined in.

Gornotsvetov gave a final pluck to the strings and stopped playing. Everyone felt awkward.

"Some singers!" Podtyagin grunted despondently, and shook his head, propped on his hand. He felt bad: the thought of his lost passport was combined with a stifling shortness of breath.

"I shouldn't drink, that's the trouble," he added glumly.

"I told you so," murmured Klara. "You're like a baby, Anton Sergeyevich."

"Why isn't anybody eating or drinking?" said Kolin, waggling his hips as he minced around the table. He began filling up empty glasses. Nobody said anything. The party, obviously, was a failure.

Ganin, who until then had been sitting on the window ledge and staring, with a faint smile of pensive irony, at the mauve glimmer of the table and the strangely lit faces, suddenly jumped down to the floor and gave a peal of clear laughter.

"Fill 'em up, Kolin," he said as he walked over to the table. "Some more for Alfyorov. Tomorrow our life changes. Tomorrow I shan't be here any longer. Come on, down the hatch. Stop looking at me like a wounded deer, Klara. Give her some more of that liqueur. You too, Anton Sergeyevich— cheer up. No good moping about your passport. You'll get another one, even better than the old one. Recite us some of your poetry. Oh yes, by the way—"

"Can I have that empty bottle?" Alfyorov said suddenly, and a lascivious gleam sparkled in his joyful, excited eyes.

"By the way," Ganin repeated, coming up behind the old man and putting his hand on his fleshy shoulder, "I remember some of your verses, Anton Sergeyevich. 'Full moon—forest and stream'—that's right, isn't it?"

Podtyagin turned and looked at him, then gave an unhurried smile. "Did you find it in an old calendar? They were very fond of printing my poetry on calendar leaves. On the underside, above the recipe for the day."

"Gentlemen, gentlemen, what is he trying to do?" shouted Kolin, pointing at Alfyorov, who, having flung open the window, had suddenly raised the bottle and was aiming it into the dark blue night.

"Let him," Ganin laughed. "Let him act up if he wants to."

Alfyorov's beard gleamed, his Adam's apple swelled and the sparse hair at his temples stirred in the night breeze. Bringing back his arm in a wide sweep, he stood still for a while and then solemnly placed the bottle on the floor.

The dancers burst into laughter.

Alfyorov sat down beside Gornotsvetov, took the guitar from him and began to try to play it. He was a man who got drunk very quickly.

"Klara's so serious-looking," Podtyagin said with difficulty. "Girls like her used to write me such moving letters. Now she doesn't want to look at me."

"Don't drink any more. Please," said Klara, thinking that she had never been so miserable in her life as now.

Podtyagin managed a forced smile and pulled at Ganin's sleeve. "Now here's the future savior of Russia. Tell us a story, Lyovushka—where did you roam, where did you fight?"

"Must I?" asked Ganin with a good-natured grimace.

"Yes, do. I feel so depressed, you know. When did you leave Russia?"

"When? Hey, Kolin. Let's have some of that sticky stuff. No, not for me—for Alfyorov. That's right. Mix it into his glass."

15

Lydia Nikolaevna was already in bed. She had nervously refused the dancers' invitation and was now sleeping an old woman's light sleep, through which the heavy vibration of the trains passed with the sound of huge cupboards full of quivering crockery. Occasionally her sleep would be broken, and then she would vaguely hear the voices in room 6. Once she dreamed of Ganin, and in her dreams she could not understand who he was and where he had come from. Indeed, his personality was surrounded by mystery. And no wonder: he never told anybody about his life, his wanderings and his adventures of recent years—even he himself remembered his escape from Russia as though in a dream, a dream that was like a faintly sparkling sea mist.

Perhaps Mary had written more letters at that time—early 1919—when he had been fighting in the northern Crimea, but he had not received them if she had. Perekop tottered and fell. Wounded in the head, Ganin had been evacuated to Simferopol; and a week later, sick and listless, cut off from his unit which had retreated to Feodosia, he had been caught up in the mad, nightmarish torrent of the civilian evacuation. In the fields and on the slopes of the Heights of Inkerman, where once the uniforms of Queen Victoria's soldiers had flashed scarlet among the smoke of toy cannon, the lovely and wild Crimean spring was already blossoming. Smoothly undulating, the milky-white road flowed on, the open cover of the car rattled as the wheels bounced over bumps and holes—and the feeling of speed, the feeling of spring, of space and the pale green of the hills, suddenly fused into a delicious joy which made it possible to forget that this light-hearted road was the way leading out of Russia.

He reached Sevastopol still full of joy, and left his suitcase at the white-stone Hotel Kist, where the confusion was indescribable. Then drunk with hazy sunshine and the dull pain in his head he set off, past the pale doric columns of the portico, down the broad granite flagstones of the steps to the harbor, and stared long at the melting blue glitter of the sea without the idea of exile once entering his head. Then he climbed back up to the square where the gray statue of Admiral Nakhimov stands in long naval frock coat, with spyglass, and wandering along the dusty white street as far as the Fourth Bastion, he visited the Panorama. Beyond the circular balustrade genuine old guns, sandbags, intentionally strewn splinters and real circuslike sand merged into a soft, smoky-blue, rather airless picture which surrounded the sightseers' platform and teased the eye with the elusiveness of its boundaries.

This was how Sevastopol remained in his memory—vernal, dusty, in the grip of a kind of lifeless, dreamy disquiet.

At night, on board ship, he watched the empty white sleeves of searchlights filling in and sinking again across the sky, while the black water looked varnished in the moonlight and farther away, in the night haze, a brightly lit foreign cruiser rode at anchor, resting on the streamy gold pillars of its own reflection.

He took passage on a shabby Greek ship; the deck was covered with rows of penniless, swarthy refugees from Eupa-

toria, where the ship had called that morning. Ganin had installed himself in the wardroom, where the lamp ponderously
swayed and the long table was piled with huge onion-shaped
bundles.

Then came several glorious, sad days at sea. Like two floating white wings the oncoming foam embraced everything,
embraced the bow of the steamer as it cut through it; and
the green shadows of people leaning on the ship's rails flick-
ered softly across the bright slopes of the waves. The rusty
steering gear creaked, two seagulls glided round the funnel
and their wet bills, caught in a ray of sunshine, flashed like
diamonds. Nearby a big-headed Greek baby began crying
and its mother lost her temper and started to spit at it in a
desperate effort to silence it. A stoker sometimes emerged on
deck, black all over, with eyes ringed with coal dust and a
fake ruby on his index finger.

It was such trivia—and not nostalgia for his abandoned
homeland—that stuck in Ganin's memory, as though only his
eyes had been alive and his mind had gone into hiding.

On the second day Istanbul loomed darkly in the orange-
colored evening and slowly dissolved in the night which
overtook the ship. At dawn Ganin climbed up onto the
bridge: the vague, dark blue outline of the Scutari shore was
gradually becoming visible. The moon's reflection narrowed
and paled. In the east the blue-mauve of the sky modulated
to a golden red, and Istanbul, shining faintly, began to float
out of the mist. A silky band of ripples glittered along the
shore; a black rowboat and a black fez sailed noiselessly past.
Now the east was turning white and a breeze sprung up
which brushed over Ganin's face with a salty tickle. From the
shore came the sound of reveille being played; two seagulls,
black as crows, flapped over the ship, and with a patter like
light rain a shoal of fish broke the surface in a network of
momentary rings. A lighter came alongside; on the water be-

neath it, its shadow extended and then retracted its tentacles. But only when Ganin stepped ashore and saw a blue-clad Turk on the quayside asleep on a mountain of oranges—only then did he feel a clear, piercing sense of how far he was from the warm mass of his own country and from Mary, whom he loved forever.

All this now unfolded in his memory, flashing disjointedly, and shrank again into a warm lump when Podtyagin, with a great effort, asked him, "How long ago did you leave Russia?"

"Five years," he answered curtly; and then, as he sat in a corner in the languorous violet light which poured over the cloth on the table in the center of the room and over the smiling faces of Kolin and Gornotsvetov, who were dancing silently and energetically in the middle of the room, Ganin thought, "What happiness! Tomorrow—no, it's today, it's already past midnight. Mary cannot have changed since then, her Tartar eyes still burn and smile just as they did." He would take her far away, he would work tirelessly for her. Tomorrow all his youth, his Russia, was coming back to him again.

Arms akimbo, throwing back his head and shaking it, now gliding, now stamping his heels and waving a handkerchief, Kolin was weaving around Gornotsvetov, who, squatting on his haunches, was nimbly and rakishly kicking his legs out quicker and quicker until he was finally revolving on one bent leg. Totally drunk, Alfyorov sat swaying with a benign expression. Klara kept glancing anxiously at Podtyagin's gray, sweating face; the old man sat in an awkward sideways position on the bed.

"You aren't well, Anton Sergeyevich," she whispered. "You should go to bed, it's around half-past one."

Oh, how simple it would be: tomorrow—no, today—he would see her again, provided Alfyorov got really tight. Only

six hours more. Right now she would be asleep in her compartment, the telegraph poles flying by in the darkness, pine
trees and hills rushing up to the train—what a noise these boys
were making. Won't they ever stop dancing? Yes, amazingly
simple—at times there was something like genius in the work-
ings of fate—

"All right, I shall go and lie down a bit," said Podtyagin
dully, and with a heavy sigh started to leave.

"Where is the grand fellow going? Stop—stay a bit longer,"
Alfyorov muttered gaily.

"Have another drink and shut up," Ganin said to Alfyorov,
then quickly joined Podtyagin. "Lean on me, Anton Sergeyevich."

The old man looked hazily at him, made a gesture as
though swatting a fly and suddenly, with a faint cry, he staggered and pitched forward.

Ganin and Klara managed to catch him in time, while the
dancers fussed around. Scarcely moving his sticky tongue,
Alfyorov blabbered with drunken callousness, "Look, look—
he's dying."

"Stop running about and do something useful, Gornotsvetov," Ganin said calmly. "Hold his head. Kolin—support him
here. No, that's my arm—higher up. Stop gaping at me like
that. Higher up, I say. Open the door, Klara."

The three of them carried the old man to his room. Stag-
gering, Alfyorov made as if to follow them, then limply
waved his hand and sat down at the table. With a shaking
hand he poured himself out some vodka, then pulled a nickel-
plated watch out of his waistcoat pocket and put it in front
of him on the table.

"Three, four, five, six, seven, eight." He drew his finger
round the Roman figures, stopped, his head turned aside, and
sat watching the second hand with one eye.

[103]

In the passage, the dachshund began yelping in a high-pitched, excited voice. Alfyorov grimaced. "Lousy little dog. Ought to be run over."

A little later he took an indelible pencil out of another pocket and smeared a mauve mark on the glass above the figure eight.

"She's coming, coming, coming," he said to himself in time with the ticking.

He glanced round the table, took a chocolate and immediately spat it out. A brown blob smacked against the wall.

"Three, four, five, seven," Alfyorov started counting again and winked at the dial with a bleary, ecstatic smile.

16

The town had grown quiet in the night. The hunched old man in the black cloak was already on the move, tapping his stick and bending over with a grunt whenever its sharp point turned up a butt-end. An occasional car drove by, and even more rarely a night droshky would jolt by with a click of hooves. A drunk in a bowler hat was waiting for a tram on the corner, although the trams had stopped running at least two hours ago. A few prostitutes were strolling up and down, yawning and talking to shady loafers with upturned coat collars. One of the girls accosted Kolin and Gornotsvetov as they advanced almost at a run, but she turned away again at once after casting a professional glance at their pale, effeminate faces.

The dancers had undertaken to fetch a Russian doctor they knew to see Podtyagin, and indeed, after an hour and a half, they returned accompanied by a sleepy-looking gentleman with stiff, clean-shaven features. He stayed for half an hour, now and again making a sucking noise as though he had a hole in his tooth, and then left.

It was now very quiet in the unlighted room. There reigned that special, heavy, dull silence which always comes when several people are sitting in silence around a sick person. The night was now waning. Ganin's profile, turned toward the bed, seemed carved out of pale blue stone; at the foot of the bed, in a vague armchair floating on the waves of the dawn, Klara sat looking fixedly in the same direction. Farther away, Gornotsvetov and Kolin huddled side by side on a little divan —and their faces were like two pale blobs.

The doctor was already going down the stairs behind the black figure of Frau Dorn, her bunch of keys chinking softly as she apologized for the lift being out of order. Reaching the bottom she opened the heavy front door and the doctor, raising his hat, departed into the bluish haze.

The old woman carefully locked the door, wrapped herself tighter in her black knitted shawl and went upstairs. The steps were lit by a cold yellow light. Her keys tinkling gently, she reached the landing. The light on the staircase went out.

In the lobby she met Ganin, who had come out of Podtyagin's room, carefully pulling the door behind him.

"The doctor has promised to come back in the morning," whispered the old woman. "How is he now—better?"

Ganin shrugged. "I don't know. I think not, though. The way he is breathing—it's a frightening sound."

Lydia Nikolaevna sighed and timidly entered the room. With an identical movement Klara and the two dancers turned their palely glistening eyes toward her and then turned back again to stare at the bed. A breeze rattled the frame of the half-open window.

Ganin walked down the passage on tiptoe and went back to the room where the party had recently taken place. As he supposed, Alfyorov was still sitting at the table. His face seemed swollen and shone gray from the combination of the light of dawn and the theatrically shaded lamp. He was nodding, occasionally belching. On the watchglass in front of him gleamed a drop of vodka in which a mauve trace of indelible pencil was spreading. Only four hours to go.

Ganin sat down beside that drunken, drowsy creature and stared long at him, knitting his thick brows and propping his temple on his clenched fist, which stretched his skin and caused his eye to slant.

Alfyorov suddenly came to life and slowly turned to look at him.

"Isn't it time you were going to bed, my dear Aleksey Ivanovich," said Ganin distinctly.

"No," Alfyorov pronounced with difficulty, and after some thought, as though solving a difficult problem, he repeated, "No."

Ganin switched off the unnecessary light, took out his cigarette case and lit a cigarette. Whether from the cold of the pale dawn or from the whiff of tobacco, Alfyorov seemed to sober up a little.

He rubbed his forehead with the palm of his hand, looked around and stretched out a fairly firm hand for a bottle.

Halfway to it his hand stopped, he shook his head, then with a slack smile said to Ganin, "Mustn't have any more. Mary's coming."

After a while he shook Ganin's arm. "Hey, you, what's your name—Leb Lebovich—d'you hear—Mary—"

Ganin exhaled the smoke and stared hard into Alfyorov's face. He took it all in at once: the wet, half-open mouth, the little dung-colored beard, the watery blinking eyes.

"Listen, Leb Lebovich"—Alfyorov swayed and grabbed him by the shoulder. "Right now I'm dead drunk, canned, tight as a drum. They made me drink, damn 'em—no, that's not it—I wanted to tell you about the girl—"

"You need a good sleep, Aleksey Ivanovich."

"There was a girl, I tell you. No, I'm not talking about my wife—my wife's pure—but I'd been so many years without my wife. So not long ago—no, it was long ago—can't remember when—girl took me up to her place. Foxy-looking little thing—such filth—and yet delicious. And now Mary's coming. D'you realize what it means? D'you realize or not? I'm drunk—can't remember how to say perp—purple—perpendicular—and Mary'll be here soon. Why did it all have to happen like this? Eh? I'm asking you! You, you damn Bolshevik! Can't you tell me why?"

Ganin gently pushed away his hand. Head nodding, Alfyorov leaned forward over the table; his elbow slipped, rumpling the tablecloth and knocking over the glasses. The glasses, a saucer and the watch slid to the floor.

"Bed," said Ganin and jerked him violently to his feet.

Alfyorov did not resist, but he was so unsteady that Ganin could hardly make him walk in the right direction.

Finding himself in his own room, he gave a broad, sleepy grin and collapsed slowly onto the bed. Suddenly horror crossed his face.

"Alarm clock—" he mumbled, sitting up. "Leb—over there, on the table, alarm clock—set it for half past seven."

"All right," said Ganin, and began moving the hand. He set it for ten o'clock, then changed his mind and set it for eleven.

When he looked at Alfyorov again the man was already sound asleep, flat on his back with one arm oddly thrown out.

This was how drunken tramps used to sleep in Russian villages. All day in the shimmering, sleepy heat tall laden carts had swayed past, scattering the country road with bits of hay—and the tramp had lurched noisily along, pestering girl vacationists, beating his resonant chest, proclaiming himself the son of a general and finally, slapping his peaked cap to the ground, he had lain down across the road, and had stayed there until a peasant climbed down from his hay wagon. The peasant had dragged him to the verge and driven on; and the tramp, turning his pale face aside, had lain like a corpse on the edge of the ditch while the great green bulks, swaying and sweet-smelling, had glided past, through the dappled shadows of the lime trees in bloom.

Putting the alarm clock noiselessly down on the table, Ganin stood for a long time looking at the sleeping man. Then jingling the money in his trouser pocket he turned and quietly went out.

In the dim little bathroom next to the kitchen, briquettes of coal were piled up under a piece of matting. The pane of the narrow window was broken, there were yellow streaks on the walls, the metal shower head curved, whiplike, out from the wall above the black, peeling bathtub. Ganin stripped naked and for several minutes stretched his arms and legs—strong, white, blue-veined. His muscles cracked and rippled. His chest breathed deeply and evenly. He turned on the tap of the shower and stood under the icy, fan-shaped stream, which produced a delicious contraction in his stomach.

Dressed again, tingling hotly all over, trying not to make any noise, he dragged his suitcases out into the hallway and looked at his watch. It was ten to six.

He threw hat and coat on top of the suitcases and slipped into Podtyagin's room.

The dancers were asleep on the divan, leaning against each other. Klara and Lydia Nikolaevna were bending over the old man. His eyes were shut, and his face, the color of dried clay, was occasionally distorted by an expression of pain. It was almost light. The trains were rumbling sleepily through the house.

As Ganin approached the bed-head, Podtyagin opened his eyes. For a moment in the abyss into which he kept falling his heart had found some shaky support. There was so much that he wanted to say—that he would never see Paris now, still less his homeland, that his whole life had been stupid and fruitless, and that he didn't know why he had lived, or why he was dying. Rolling his head to one side and glancing perplexedly at Ganin he muttered, "You see—without any passport." Something like faint mirth twisted his lips. He screwed up his eyes again and once more the abyss sucked him down, a wedge of pain drove itself into his heart—and to breathe air seemed to be unspeakable, unattainable bliss.

Ganin, gripping the edge of the bed with a strong white hand, looked in the old man's face, and once again he remembered these flickering, shadowy doppelgängers, the casual Russian film extras, sold for ten marks apiece and still flitting, God knows where, across the white gleam of a screen. It occurred to him that Podtyagin nevertheless had bequeathed something, even if nothing more than the two pallid verses which had blossomed into such warm, undying life for him, Ganin, in the same way as a cheap perfume or the street signs in a familiar street become dear to us. For a moment he saw life in all the thrilling beauty of its despair and happiness, and everything became exalted and deeply mysterious—his own past, Podtyagin's face bathed in pale light, the blurred reflection of the window frame on the blue wall and the two women in dark dresses standing motionless beside him.

Klara noticed with amazement that Ganin was smiling, and she could not understand it.

Smiling, he touched Podtyagin's hand, which barely twitched as it lay on the sheet, straightened up and turned to Frau Dorn and Klara.

"I'm leaving now," he whispered. "I don't suppose we shall meet again. Give my regards to the dancers."

"I'll see you out," said Klara as quietly, and added, "The dancers are asleep on the divan."

And Ganin went out of the room. In the lobby he picked up his suitcases and threw his mackintosh over his shoulder, and Klara opened the door for him.

"Thank you very much," he said, sidling out onto the landing. "Good luck."

For a moment he stopped. Already the day before he had momentarily thought it would be a good idea to explain to Klara that he had never had any intention of stealing money but had been looking at old photographs; yet now he could not remember what he had meant to say. So with a bow he set off unhurriedly down the staircase. Klara, holding the door handle, watched him go. He carried his suitcases like buckets and his heavy footfalls made a noise on the stairs like a slow heartbeat. Long after he had disappeared round the turn of the banisters she stood and listened to that steady, diminishing tap. Finally she shut the door, stood for a moment in the hallway. She repeated aloud, "The dancers are asleep on the divan," and suddenly burst into soundless but violent sobs, running her index finger up and down the wall.

17

The thick, heavy hands on the huge white clockface that projected sideways from a watchmaker's sign showed twenty-four minutes to seven. In the faint blue of the sky that had still not warmed up after the night, only one small cloud had begun to turn pink, and there was an unearthly grace about its long, thin outline. The footsteps of those unfortunates who were up and about at this hour rang out with especial clarity in the deserted air and in the distance a fleshy pink light quivered on the tram tracks. A small cart, loaded with enormous bunches of violets half covered with a coarse striped cloth, moved slowly along close to the curb, the flower-seller helping a large red-haired dog to pull it. Its tongue hanging out, the dog was straining forward, exerting every one of its sinewy muscles devoted to man.

From the black branches of some trees, just beginning to sprout green, a flock of sparrows fluttered away with an airy rustle and settled on the narrow ledge of a high brick wall.

The shops were still asleep behind their iron grilles, the houses as yet sunlit only from above, but it would have been impossible to imagine that this was sunset and not early morning. Because the shadows lay the wrong way, unexpected combinations met the eye accustomed to evening shadows but unfamiliar with auroral ones.

Everything seemed askew, attenuated, metamorphosed as in a mirror. And just as the sun rose higher and the shadows dispersed to their usual places, so in that sober light the world of memories in which Ganin had dwelt became what it was in reality: the distant past.

He looked round and saw at the end of the street the sunlit corner of the house where he had been reliving his past and to which he would never return again. There was something beautifully mysterious about the departure from his life of a whole house.

As the sun rose higher and higher and the city grew lighter, in step with it, the street came to life and lost its strange shadowy charm. Ganin walked down the middle of the sidewalk, gently swinging his solidly packed bags, and thought how long it was since he had felt so fit, strong and ready to tackle anything. And the fact that he kept noticing everything with a fresh, loving eye—the carts driving to market, the slender, half-unfolded leaves and the many-colored posters which a man in an apron was sticking around a kiosk—this fact meant a secret turning point for him, an awakening.

He stopped in the little public garden near the station and sat on the same bench where such a short while ago he had remembered typhus, the country house, his presentiment of Mary. In an hour's time she would be coming, her husband was sleeping the sleep of the dead and he, Ganin, was about to meet her.

For some reason he suddenly remembered how he had gone to say goodbye to Lyudmila, how he had walked out of her room.

Behind the public garden a house was being built; he could see the yellow wooden framework of beams—the skeleton of the roof, which in parts was already tiled.

Despite the early hour, work was already in progress. The figures of the workmen on the frame showed blue against the morning sky. One was walking along the ridge-piece, as light and free as though he were about to fly away. The wooden frame shone like gold in the sun, while on it two workmen were passing tiles to a third man. They lay on their backs, one above the other in a straight line as if on a staircase. The lower man passed the red slab, like a large book, over his head; the man in the middle took the tile and with the same movement, leaning right back and stretching out his arms, passed it on up to the workman above. This lazy, regular process had a curiously calming effect; the yellow sheen of fresh timber was more alive than the most lifelike dream of the past. As Ganin looked up at the skeletal roof in the ethereal sky he realized with merciless clarity that his affair with Mary was ended forever. It had lasted no more than four days—four days which were perhaps the happiest days of his life. But now he had exhausted his memories, was sated by them, and the image of Mary, together with that of the old dying poet, now remained in the house of ghosts, which itself was already a memory.

Other than that image no Mary existed, nor could exist.

He waited for the moment when the express from the north slowly rolled across the iron bridge. It passed on and disappeared behind the façade of the station.

Then he picked up his suitcases, hailed a taxi and told the driver to go to a different station at the other end of the city. He chose a train leaving for southwestern Germany in half an hour, spent a quarter of his whole fortune on the ticket and thought with pleasurable excitement how he would cross the frontier without a single visa; and beyond it was France, Provence, and then—the sea.

As his train moved off he fell into a doze, his face buried in the folds of his mackintosh, hanging from a hook above the wooden seat.